GYM CLASS KLUTZ

CAROL LYNN LUCK

For Marin —
Play to your strengths and enjoy everything you do. Don't let anyone get you down —
Carol

ISBN-13: 978-1518627170

This novel is based, in part, on actual events. The names, characters, and incidents are products of the author's imagination or are used fictitiously. Any similarity of these fictitious characters to the name, attributes or actual background of any person, living or dead, is coincidental and unintentional.

Printed by CreateSpace Store Address:
www.createspace.com/5608812

Available from Amazon.com, CreateSpace.com and other retail outlets

http://www.CarolLynnLuck.com
@Luckwrites
Facebook.com/Carol Lach

This book is dedicated
to the teachers
whose lessons last the rest of our lives,

and

to the students
who persevere in spite of failings—
you will triumph.

TABLE of CONTENTS

1. PAGE HIGH SCHOOL

The bus screeches to a stop.

"Hey, Girl," the driver yells as he jumps out, "watch where you're going!"

I watch kids pouring out of the long line of orange school buses and trampling the grass as they swarm inside the sprawling brick building. Silver letters that spell out "John C. Page High School" gleam in the sunlight. The year, 1962, is etched in stone near the bottom of the same wall, reminding me of a tombstone.

How will I ever find my way to my classes? Will my teachers send me to the office for being late? Will high school be hard? Will I be able to make friends? These questions race through my mind as my cold, clammy hands grip the handle on my purse. This is exciting, and scary! I don't know a single person, and I don't know what to expect.

"Kid, you've got to be more careful," the bus driver is saying to a girl in a red sweater. "I coulda' hit you—lucky thing the brakes are good."

"All right! All right!" she shouts back at him without stopping.

Watching out the window, something seems familiar about her. I wait for everyone else to get off the bus only because I'd rather be last than get pushed and trip.

At the front door, a tall man in a brown suit welcomes me and hands me a map of the school. I look at the paper carefully, trying to find a pattern to the room numbers in this huge building. On the walls names are posted by grade with homeroom numbers next to them. I look for the freshman list, find Kenda next to my last name with the number 204. Kids are pushing and shoving from every direction. Feeling lost in the mob, I decide to go up the nearest flight of stairs, assuming that 204 is on the second floor. When I get to the top, I find a clearing in the hallway, study the map, get to my homeroom and sigh with relief.

A little round-faced teacher greets me with a friendly "*Bonjour*". This is a French class, with Monsieur LeCourt written in neat script on the board. But he looks more like an Irish leprechaun. With only a few other students in the room, he asks our names and gives us our schedules. I reply with a quiet "Merci" as I take a seat off to the side in the second row. On my schedule, the name next to French is not LeCourt—I guess I won't have the cheery leprechaun for French.

Other kids pour into the room, talking, laughing and joking around. The Leprechaun welcomes them and finishes passing out schedules. As I look around the room, I don't see a single familiar face. How I wish we lived in a neighborhood like normal people. Instead we are way out in the country between three towns.

There's the girl in the red sweater who almost got hit by our bus driver. She's arguing with a boy sitting in the desk by the door. Monsieur LeCourt walks down the aisles. As he sets a brown card on each student's desk, he smiles, asks if they enjoyed the summer or comments on our brand new school.

"These cards have your locker numbers and combinations along with directions on how to open them. If you need help with your locker or anything else, you know where to find me."

The bell rings and I head for the gym through thick, noisy crowds. Nearly everyone is going in the opposite direction. I feel like a salmon swimming upstream. Finally, the gym is in sight. On the door, a hand-written note says "Girls go to room 112".

Checking my map, I move quickly around the corner, find the room, and take my seat in the second row off to the side. The teacher is standing in front of large blackboards that cover the front wall. She's only a few inches taller than me, but stocky and muscular with short brown hair. Her solid stance projects power. There are about thirty wooden chairs with small desktops attached and wire racks below the seats. One shiny poster shows a food pyramid and another says, "Smoking may be hazardous to your health."

Coming in the door is the girl in the red sweater. I think I know her. She looks like Mary Sue Parsonfield, who used to live next door to us before we moved to the country.

Oh no, *please*, anyone else in the whole world but her!

She slams her loose-leaf binder down on the desk next to mine and I jump! What did I do? I look at her face. She is seething with anger, but it couldn't be my fault. I haven’t seen her in four years.

"Now that you've got everyone's attention, what's your name?" the teacher barks, breaking the silence.

"Mary Sue,” she replies belligerently, tossing her long blond hair over her shoulder. She’s slim and pretty, except for her attitude.

"Mary Sue who? This is gym class! You will use your last name, just like in the military!"

"Parsonfield" Mary Sue growls.

“Parsonfield, what?”

“Huh? That’s all,” Mary Sue says. “Isn’t it long enough?”

“I mean, how do you address a teacher? My name is on the board.”

“Yeah, I can read. Miss Ditch,” Mary Sue mutters.

"Okay Parsonfield, you need to walk out of this room, come back in, set your book down properly and act your age."

She stomps out of the room. Seconds pass, one... two... three... four... five... six... seven... eight… nine. Mary Sue saunters in the door, her hips swaying, pausing and posing like an actress, waving her free arm with two fingers holding an imaginary cigarette. As she sets her binder on the desk and takes off her red sweater, she glares at me.

Does she recognize me? Or is she just mad at the world?

Other girls giggle; I don’t dare. I don’t want any trouble, not on my very first day of high school.

Miss Ditch looks straight at Mary Sue. “Now what exactly is the problem here?" she asks in a booming voice.

"Gym class first thing in the morning—it's the pits!" Mary Sue replies. "I'll be all sweaty and smelly the whole day, not to mention what my hair will look like." She poofs up the top of her blond hair with the palm of her hand, showing off her red–polished nails.

Miss Ditch's voice breaks through the spirited chatter. "As y'all know by now I'm Miss Ditch and that starts with a 'D'. I'll be your health and P.E. teacher this year and you need to know from the start that I run a tight ship."

As she rambles on, I think, it's more like Miss *Witch.*

"Let's get on with roll call. Then I'll go over how things work around here."

"Lowery"

"Here"

"Lyman"

"Here"

On and on, name after name it goes.

"Nickelfen.. Nickelfens.. or Nickelfensen? Now that's a mouthful. How about we just go with Nick?"

"Uh, okay, Miss Ditch," says a girl with long, shiny blond hair. She moves her raised hand to her side as gracefully as a ballerina.

I can tell by her tone that she doesn't like it, but what choice does she have? *Yuck*, I think, *that's a boy's name and she's so pretty.* I suddenly begin to dread Miss Ditch calling my name. Already I feel my palms getting sweaty as I rub my hands together.

"Norwood"

“Here”

“Panic? Is that right?”

Giggles and snickers come from all around. Everyone looks at me.

I look down at my desk, pretending I'm invisible.

Quietly I answer, "Yes, Miss Ditch. P-A-N-N-E-K is pronounced panic."

The booming voice replies, "I can't hear you. While you're at it why don't you tell us where a name like that came from.”

"Yes, Miss Ditch you pronounced it right,” I repeat a little louder without looking up. “It's Polish,” I add.

Memories of third grade rush into my head. Kids running up to me in the playground acting like ghosts and vampires, humming that spooky tune from the TV show “Panic”. Before then I thought Pannek was just my name.

More giggles, and then someone whispers, “Yeah that’s gotta be right. Only a dumb Pollak would have a name like that!”

Can’t we start this class all over again? Pretend it’s a good day and not a nightmare?

Miss Ditch’s voice brings me back to the present, "Okay, moving right along. Parsonfield, we all know *you're* here."

“Poison, with two ‘s’s.”

“It’s pronounced Pwassown. It’s French, Miss Ditch. And I’m here.”

“Thank you for the clarification. Poison is a lot easier and it’s English. In case you hadn’t noticed, we speak English here.”

I guess that means she’ll be called Poison all year in this class. It means fish, I almost wonder which is worse, fish or poison. A military boot camp is not what I expected for high school. I sure hope the teachers in my other classes are more like 'Mr. Leprechaun'.

Finally, roll call is done.

"We have health here every other day and PE—physical education—on the alternate ones. When we have PE, you will go directly to the locker room, dress, and report to the gym or the field in nice weather. You get a point each day for dressing out. That means in your gym suit, white socks and tennis shoes. At the end of class when you return to the locker room, you take a towel and head for the showers. When you come out of the shower, wrapped in your towel, I will be standing at the door to give you another check. There are a few private showers reserved for the girls who have their periods. You will have seven minutes to shower and get ready for your next class. That should be plenty, but you can't dally."

Miss Ditch continues, "Now we understand that some of you may be very athletic and others not at all. Since this is something you're born with, we want to make it possible for those without talent and even the downright clumsy ones to pass this course. Your grade will be determined: 50% health tests, 10% checks for dressing out and showering, 10% for your sports rules tests and 30% for your skills tests. Your rules tests will include the history of the sport, dimensions of the field or court, how the scoring is done and how it's played. Of course, we reserve the right to take off points for unsportsmanlike conduct and any other infractions as we see fit. Any questions?"

This is not a good beginning for me. Somehow, I know I meet her definition of “downright clumsy”. I have an awful feeling in the pit of my stomach that my embarrassment in this class has just begun. At least we’ll only have gym half the time, I think, trying to make myself feel better.

The booming voice brings me back to the present nightmare.

“Now, in health class we will be covering diseases, nutrition, childbirth and sex education, including sexually transmitted diseases, Gonorrhea and Syphilis. You'll see a movie on childbirth, which we hear is the best advertisement for abstinence. Then we’ll cover drug abuse as well as safety and first aid."

"For your gym uniforms, you will be responsible for bringing your own white socks and white tennis shoes and fifteen dollars tomorrow. When you enter the locker room, we will exchange your money for a uniform, which looks like this."

She holds up this hideous blue one-piece uniform. It snaps up the front, has short sleeves, a belt, a collar, and worst of all bloomers. We all groan.

This is absolutely gross. I suppose the looks of my gym suit will be the farthest thing from my mind when I'm trying to pretend I'm coordinated in this class. At least everyone else in here has to wear them, and there are no boys to see us. Small consolations; take them when you can.

Miss Ditch continues, "You will be responsible for keeping your uniform clean and pressed. Every weekend, you will be expected to take it home, and wash it. There is not enough deodorant in the universe to cover the smell of a two-week old dirty gym suit, even though it will be worn less than an hour a day. You *will* sweat in here or you won't pass."

On and on she talks. Nothing she says is good news to me.

Will this class never end?

Bzzzzt! The bell at last.

2. MORE CLASSES

Next I go to Geometry class. I look at my map, hoping it's close. Yikes! It's upstairs in the opposite corner of the building.

"How long is four minutes?" I ask to no one in particular.

The hallways are a real mob scene; kids are shoving, pushing, and shouting. I get smashed against the wall and the only way out is to duck and slither along. This is one time when it's good to be short and thin. The stairs are really packed and again, I find myself going the wrong way—up, when all the world is coming down. As I inch along, I wonder what the consequences will be for getting to class late. Just as I step in the door, the bell rings.

There are two seats left in the front row and one in the very back. Quickly I slip into the closest one in the front and catch my breath. The blackboard is clean with crisp, neat white lettering. It says "Captain Wilson. Welcome to Geometry." Oh no, more military, it's awful living close to Washington D.C. I sure hope he doesn't run a tight ship like Miss Ditch. He smiles and speaks loudly, but there is a kindness in his voice.

"Good morning class! I hope you are having a nice day in this wonderful brand new school. As I take roll, please say if you are a sophomore or a freshman."

It's interesting to know how many other freshman are in here, so I open my binder to a blank page, draw a line down the center, put a "*S*" at the top of one side, and "*F*" on the other. I make tally marks in the two columns as kids answer. This also keeps roll call from being too boring. I almost forget to answer when Captain Wilson calls my name.

The teacher proceeds to pass out textbooks and record the numbers in each on a list at his desk. Kids are all talking to friends but I don't know anyone in here. I try to smile at the girl sitting next to me, but she turns to the good-looking dude on the other side and starts up an animated conversation with him. When my name is called I go up and get my brand new book and open it. Even the smell is fresh, inky and leathery.

The Captain passes out the last book and slides his hand through his light brown hair. Then he stands tall and tells us that he has only a few rules. No talking when someone else is, especially if a fellow student is explaining his or her work at the board. Do not make fun of anyone who makes a mistake, the next error on the board could be yours. Do your homework. It is impossible to pass Geometry unless you practice.

I am looking through my book thinking good grief! Am I really going to learn all this before the school year ends?

The Captain shows us how geometry isn't just about math calculations and explains what a proof is. It reminds me of the mysteries you have to solve with just a few clues. I love puzzles, so I might actually enjoy this class.

Soon geometry will be over. I look at my schedule and map and try to figure out how to get to French class. When the bell rings, I look at all the kids filing out of the room, mostly boys.

How I wish I had a friend, or knew someone, besides Mary Sue.

French class is in room 207 with Froid. That's close to my homeroom, so I know how to get there. The main part of the school is two large squares, once you learn the numbers at the corners it should be easy, except for the vocational-tech wing. I don't think I'll be having any classes there anyway.

Better stop at the girl's bathroom before lunch or I'll never make it through the day. Rushing in the door, I almost choke on the thick smoke. I have to get past girls standing by the sinks. One is teasing her hair with a comb, trying to make it look all fluffed up. Another is putting on bright red lipstick while the third applies tons of moldy green colored eye shadow. The tallest one sweeps her arm gracefully holding a lit cigarette; her bright red nail polish is easily visible through the thick smog. They all freeze, sigh with relief and then glare at me.

"What do you think you're doing in here?" the tall one asks.

"I just need to use the bathroom," my squeaky voice replies.

"Oh, the little girl's got to pee, Huh? Well, hurry it up and get out of here. You say one word to anyone about this and you'll know what the tip of a lit cigarette feels like. Ya got it, Shrimp?"

I am so scared I almost wet my pants before I get into the stall. On the way out, I rush past them.

The tall one snarls, "remember, one word to anyone, and you'll get a tattoo with a lit cigarette. I promise. And I have witnesses."

Across the hall is the cafeteria. I pull out my two quarters for lunch, but it feels like the line is moving two baby steps a minute. Lunch period will be over by the time I sit down. Finally I get my lunch and see a girl in my homeroom so I go over and sit next to her.

"Hi, I'm Cathy. You're in my homeroom, aren't you?" she asks, pushing her headband back into her straight black hair. I like her matching green headband and her green plaid kilt.

"Yes, I'm Kenda."

"So how's your first day going?" she speaks casually.

"Okay, except for the girls bathroom and gym. That Miss Ditch is really tough and I have her first period."

"Oh, I have her, too," Cathy says. "She comes off like a drill sergeant, but I think she'll mellow as the year goes on. Didn't she tell your class that this year the whole school has to do President Kennedy's Physical Fitness Program? The Phys. Ed. Department feels pressured to make a name for our new school since we have no football or other sports team record to fall back on. And what happened in the bathroom?"

"A bunch of girls were in there smoking and they threatened me if I told on them. Of course, I'd never think of saying anything to a teacher, but they *were* pretty scary!"

"You better eat since there's only five minutes left of lunch period."

My chicken is tough, the green beans are almost brown, the roll is stale and the rice is sticky. Blah! But I'm so hungry, I eat as fast as I can swallow, barely chewing my food. Cathy picks up her tray, waves bye, and goes off to her next class. I brush the crumbs off my turquoise box-pleated skirt and matching printed blouse before I head for art class. It was so nice to have someone to talk to at lunch.

Art class is really relaxing and fun with Mr. Tasche. He speaks in loud whisper when he demonstrates a technique, so everyone is quiet when he talks. He twirls the ends of his handlebar mustache between his thumb and forefinger as he wanders around the room looking at our work. We are free to carry on conversations as we draw. Even with our first sketches, you can tell some kids are really good artists, like Margy, the girl sitting next to me.

3. SURVIVING THE REST OF THE FIRST DAY

My last class is up on the second floor about as far away from the art room as one can get. I race out of the room into a sea of rushing bodies and noise. *Find a stairway, quick*, I think as I try to squeeze my little thin self through the mob. "Ouch!" An elbow sticks into my ribs. Pushing onward, up the stairs I creep, oops, missed the step.

"Get outta the way, pipsqueak! What are you doing here anyway? This is high school, not second grade," a gruff, impatient voice cuts through the crowd.

I try to ignore the big bulky guy and grab for the handrail. Pulling myself up, I realize that I tore a big hole in my stocking and my shiny black dressy shoes are scuffed. Can't worry about that now, I have to get to English class. The crowd thickens and I stretch my neck as I stand on my tip-toes trying to catch a glimpse of a room number. My English teacher, Mrs. Anders paces by the door in front of her room as if she's bored and can't wait for the bell. She smiles as I approach.

"Did you just come from the gym?" she asks.

Do I look and smell that bad? I think as I try to sniff under my arm, pretending to rearrange my purse strap.

"No, art class. It's way down by the voc-tech wing."

"That's okay, I'll understand if you have a hard time getting here before the bell."

As if on cue, the bell buzzes.

Walking in the room, I head straight for the seat in the front row by the window. Good luck for a change. The girl sitting next me swishes her long brown ponytail and smiles with recognition. I smile back and begin to relax, remembering her blue vest and red plaid skirt when she got on the bus.

Attendance is taken again, but this time I recognize a few names, and learn that the girl next to me is Sharon. A few kids turn to look at me when Mrs. Anders calls "Panic", and I answer with Kenda.

"What a pretty name" she replies.

I nod and smile, even though I think it's corny. I'd prefer a normal girl's name like Linda or Sue, but my parents were expecting a boy to call Kenneth and hadn't even thought about what they'd name a girl.

Soon, Mrs. Anders passes out our literature books and tells us about the freshman English course.

"It's extremely important that you learn not only literature, but also how to write. Each week, you will write on a given topic or style—only one paragraph. You may think this is easy, but writing one convincing or descriptive paragraph is a lot harder than a full essay. It requires you to choose your words carefully and convey meaning and feeling succinctly."

My eyes drift out the window at the bright blue sky and down to the line of buses, waiting to take us home. It's hard to think of anything but finishing this long day. *Let's see 180 days times 4 years is 720, so I have 719 days of high school to go! That seems like forever.*

Mrs. Anders writes a long list of numbers on the board.

"This is the order of the buses starting by the library," she explains. "Bus #12 is the first in line and the first to leave."

Sharon turns to me. "That's us!" she says. "We've gotta hurry! No time to go to our lockers."

"Bye!" she shouts over her shoulder to the teacher, her ponytail and the blue ribbon fly in the air, as if barely attached to her head.

I try to keep up with her and make my way to the stairs, down, up, down, my head bobs as I look at the step, the blue-ribboned ponytail, the stair again almost in a rhythm. I concentrate so hard that all the chaos around me becomes a bright, noisy blur. If I don't look at each step carefully, I'll go sliding down on my butt. Finally I get to the bottom and plant both my feet on the floor. When I look up, the blue-ribboned ponytail is nowhere in sight. *I'll certainly miss my bus. Dad will find me on the dark green grass in front of the school after dark. No Stop! Think! Look around.*

"There you are! Come on! Hurry up!" I feel relief at the sound of Sharon's voice as she grabs my arm and pulls me through the crowd, and out the front doors. Ah! Fresh air! We make a dash for the first bus. Sharon jumps on, and I follow, almost crying with relief.

The bus driver frowns and shakes his bald head at me.

He asks, "Are you sure you're a high schooler, little one?"

Even the bus driver thinks I don't belong. At least he didn't call me a pipsqueak.

"I won't leave without you. She wouldn't let me." He says, as he tilts his head in the direction of the seat right behind him.

There's my sister, Annie. She's only a year older than me, but as usual, she is unruffled, her light blue blouse as fresh as when she ironed it, and not a mark on her new saddle shoes. I want to drop my stuff and hug her! The girl sitting next to Annie just smiles. I look for the closest seat and walk past Sharon.

"Thanks. I would have missed the bus without you," I whisper to Sharon and hope she knows how much I mean it.

Finally I plop my butt in an empty seat, take a deep breath, and relax for the ride home.

Well, that was some crazy day. I can't decide which was worse: scary Miss Ditch or the four girls smoking in the bathroom.

I am barely aware of the bus stopping and kids getting off. Even if I don't have any good friends at school yet, I am lucky to have Annie for a big sister. She has always been there for me. The hours and hours of household chores, garden work, cleaning the chicken coop, and selling corn at the end of the road to make money for school clothes don't seem so bad with Annie. She's a year ahead of me. I can't wait to get off the bus so we can talk on the long walk home.

4. WALKING HOME

Jim's been in Annie's class since fourth grade and he lives in the house at the end of our road. When Jim leaps off the bus his dark brown hair flies up in the front. Annie steps off and waits patiently as I grab the handrail and look down carefully at the first step, one foot down, then the other. Next the second step, cautiously, I do the same. Ah! Solid ground beneath my feet. I step forward looking down at the reddish brown dirt and gravel.

"Kennie, why does it always take you so long to get on and off the bus?"

"I don't know, guess I'm just afraid of tripping."

Jim has already dashed to his house and gone inside, without so much as a "Bye."

But then, he's one of those mysterious creatures—boys. They make no sense and follow no rules as far as I can tell. How can Annie say she wishes we had an older brother?

Annie steps up beside me. "Looks like you had a rough day," she says, "How did you tear your stocking? I told you to wear your socks and new shoes instead of your party shoes."

"Oh, Annie, *everyone* is wearing saddle shoes or penny loafers, and Mom made me get those brown tie shoes because that was all they had in my size. They are boys' shoes—and ugly."

"Just wear them and consider yourself lucky you don't have to wear my old ones."

"Yeah, easy for you to say in your bobby socks and saddle shoes. But ugly shoes are the least of my worries."

"What do you mean?"

"I have the meanest witch for health and gym in the whole world. Her name is Miss Ditch, and you'll never guess who's in that class with me! Mary Sue Parsonfield! Can you believe she showed up at our school? She had to sit next to me, and she's grown even meaner since the day I fell off her swing. Also, I don't have any gym shoes and I need fifteen dollars for one of those awful gym suits. The other really horrible thing is going to the bathroom by the cafeteria. This gang of four girls threatened to burn me with their cigarettes if I told on them for smoking."

"You didn't go in there alone, did you?"

"Yeah, I don't know a soul in this whole huge school, except Mary Sue!" A tear starts to drip down my cheek.

Annie reaches over and gives me a half-hug with her free arm.

"It's okay, Kennie. Things will get better, I promise you. I didn't know anyone at McLean High when I started last year, but now I have lots of friends. Besides, think about all those military kids who move every few years, sometimes to the other end of the earth. They never know where they'll be and they have to make new friends. And don't worry about Mary Sue. She's got a lot more problems than we'll ever have. She must have been left back 'cause she's my age, remember?"

"I guess," I grumble, "but it was still a pretty crummy day."

"Something good must have happened. I know you must have a least one teacher you like," Annie says trying to cheer me up.

"Well, my homeroom teacher is this nice little leprechaun of a guy, and my geometry, art, English and history teachers are pretty good too."

"So that's more than half. Your homeroom teacher isn't Monsieur LeCourt, is it?"

"Yes, how did you know?"

Annie continues, "I have him for French, and you're right. He'd certainly make a great little leprechaun."

Annie pauses, then gets back to her earlier question. "You still didn't tell me how you tore your stocking."

"Doesn't really matter." I change the subject and ask, "So how are your classes?"

"Pretty good. I have this cool, really tall drama teacher. He'd make a perfect Ichabod Crane."

"Who do you have for Gym and Geometry?" I ask.

"Miss Walls and Captain Wilson. Captain Wilson is nice; he's built just like Mr. Wilson in the 'Dennis the Menace' comic strip."

We both laugh.

"Yeah I know, I have Captain Wilson for geometry too. You're so lucky you don't have the Ditch," I say, spitting out her name.

"The other girls call Miss Walls Amazon lady cause she's tall, big, muscular and kind of intimidating," Annie replies.

"My classes are all interesting," Annie continues. "But I wish I had known that there were more options. Some of my friends are taking Russian, Chinese and business. Our home room teacher said that some parents complained to the superintendent about their kids having to go to a vocational school, so he promised them that our high school would have both a voc tech program and the best academic offerings anywhere."

We trudge up the steep hill, gravel crunching beneath our feet. Looking down at my dusty shoes I am reminded of how I'll have to wear the ugly brown ones tomorrow. I don't have another pair of stockings, but it'll be faster to get ready for gym with socks on. Annie reaches in her black purse, pulls out her key, and unlocks the cellar door.

We take off our dusty shoes, glad that they are not all muddy. I get the "shoe-shine kit", and take a polishing rag out of the wooden box Dad made. Quickly we both use old torn pieces of T-shirt to clean off our shoes, leave them on the rack by the door, and then go down the dark hallway into the rec room. We set our books on our desks and head upstairs to change our clothes. It's Tuesday so we have the chickens, the laundry and dinner. I volunteer to do the chickens, since Annie hates to collect the eggs and I hate to hang out laundry. It's such a waste of time; everyone else we know has a clothes dryer. Annie pulls the basket of dirty laundry out of the hall closet. We go down the stairs together. She is always at least two steps ahead of me. I have to look at each stair and hold the handrail. That's another thing I hate about the laundry; it's hard to carry the basket and see the steps.

I find Annie's old grungy school shoes from last year, they are still a little big on me, but they stay on my feet when I skip partway down the hill to the chicken coop swinging the egg basket by the handle.

I love these sunny days, they remind me that there's a world far away from Miss Ditch and the girls in the bathroom.

I stop at the apple tree and reach up to see if the green apples are as big as my fist. This is the best and only apple tree where the fruit is close enough to the ground to pick without a ladder. I can't wait until these apples are ripe; they are crispy, juicy and crunchy. Red delicious is definitely a good name for them.

When I reach the chicken coop, I carefully move the latch and open the door. The white hens move out of my way as I start pushing the scraper like a broom and the greenish brown poop makes little rows. When you do this often enough, it doesn't get too high and you can just shove it out the small side openings. The smell isn't too bad. It's a lot better than the bathroom sometimes. The big windows covered with chicken wire let a cool breeze in. I keep scraping, until the last of the chicken poop is gone. Then I grab the big scoop, dunk it into the sack of chicken feed that smells like cornbread and pour the feed into the big metal containers. They still have plenty of water until tomorrow.

Now where did I leave the egg basket?

Quickly I scan the floor and then look up. I find it hanging on the nail by the door. With the basket in hand, on tiptoe I sneak over to the nests. I reach under the first bird and snatch her egg. She squawks at me, stands up and flaps her wings. She looks down and sees the empty nest, jumps down and pecks at the food. I move to the next chicken and she treats me the same way. The third one is even noisier.

Finally I place the last egg in the basket and head for the door. Closing the latch, I see the mean old rooster, a nasty, dirty-white creature with a blood-red crown and a flying feathery tail.

If we turn our back on him he jumps up on our shoulders and digs in his claws. So I take one step at a time backwards up the hill, being ever so careful not to take my eyes off him. Trying to judge how far the basement door is, I keep going slowly, one baby step at a time while balancing the basket so the eggs don't bump against each other and crack. Then I hear the door open behind me. It must be Annie. She steps in front of me with a basket of wet clothes and waves a pillowcase at Nasty.

"Squawk! Squawk!" Half flying and half running on his two skinny legs the rooster takes off behind the coop, flapping his wings and making an awful racket. Phew! I hurry in the cellar door with the eggs, almost fill an egg carton, and take them upstairs to the fridge.

Then I look at Mom's note:

Take out the pot roast left-overs and cut the meat into cubes. Add peas and corn to the stew and Heat it up for dinner.

I go to the bathroom and wash my hands half-way up my arms, to clean off any trace of chicken poop. When I get back to the kitchen, Annie is coming in the back door.

"So what's for dinner?"

"Pot roast. If you cut up the meat, I'll get the rest of the vegetables out of the freezer and set the table."

"Sounds like a deal to me," Annie replies.

Once we have dinner all set, I find my old gym shoes from last year. They are a bit worn, but no holes. Still, I have to ask my parents for gym suit money.

"Annie, do you need money for your gym suit tomorrow?"

"No, actually we have health, so Thursday is when we need our gym suits."

"Oh. Well I need the $15 for tomorrow. I hate to ask Mom and Dad for money." I look at her hoping she'll take the hint.

Annie smiles. "Yes, Kennie, I know. I always have to do the asking. Someday, you'll have to grow up and speak for yourself."

"Yeah, I know, but not till after tonight, okay?"

5. BONNIE'S HOME

The crunch of car tires on the gravel road is loud, even through the walls. Then the car doors slam, and we hear voices. Dad is speaking until Mom raises her voice at my little sister.

"Bonnie, don't leave your stuff in the car," Mom commands.

Dad tries not to yell at Bonnie, but I know she gets on his nerves as much as Mom's. I don't even have to look out the window to know she's hopping out of the car, running off to find the kittens, paying no attention to anyone.

Her nickname should be Bouncy Brat.

The back door swings open. Bonnie jumps up the few steps, her head of short blond curls flying, and her dress all wrinkled with the top button missing. Her new shoes are all dirty, and one sock is halfway down like a flag at half-mast.

"Hey, guess what?" Bonnie shouts, "We played dodge ball at recess and I won! We colored dumb pictures, too, so I made my cow orange. I don't think the teacher liked it, but who cares? Matthew thought it was funny."

Mom comes in and tells Bonnie to wash up for dinner. Bonnie whines, skipping through the small living room.

Her little feet suddenly stop on the gray carpet and she calls out, "Hey, Kennie, come with me!"

"Why should I?" I ask. "You are perfectly capable of going to the bathroom and washing your hands by yourself."

"Suppose I don't wanna?" Bonnie whines.

"Oh, just do it and don't torture me."

"I'm not torturing you."

"Just shut up and go wash your hands." I surprise myself at how loud my voice sounds.

Mom interrupts impatiently, "Kenneee, will you two stop scrapping? She's not in the door two minutes and you're going at it. You are ten years older than Bonnie, so don't argue with her."

"I am so tired of everyone always doing whatever *she* wants. Bossy, Bratty Bonnie." I say under my breath.

"Mommy! Mommy! Kennie's calling me names."

"Kenneee, *please.* Just take her to the bathroom to wash her hands."

I want to grab her two hands and stick them under the faucet, but I restrain myself, and just stand there watching her take the soap, turn on the water and mush her hands around. The slippery soap pops out of her hands, hits the side of the sink and lands on the floor.

"Pick it up for me," Bonnie whines, *"pretty please."*

If I don't she'll be fussing again, blaming me, and Mom will be back in here, mad at *me*, of course. Slowly I reach down and take the slimy soap between my fingers. I put it in the dish next to the sink and rinse my hands.

Bonnie snatches the towel just as I reach for it to dry my hands. She may not have a clue what the word *torture* means, but she delights in it.

Mom calls to us, "girls, let's go, while dinner's still hot."

Bonnie jumps up into her chair and says, "Kennie was mean and took the towel right out of my hand when I went to use it."

Oh, here she goes again trying to get me into trouble. I say nothing. I just serve myself and start eating.

"Kennie, why can't you two get along? The best book on child-rearing by Dr. Benjamin Spock says that when children are the youngest and are used to getting lots of parental attention, they become jealous of a younger sibling who is born later and takes the attention away. Is this what the problem is?" Mom asks.

"Mom, why do you always say that? I don't know who Dr. Spock is, but as far as I'm concerned, he's wrong! I don't care if he did write that stupid book. It's not the Bible. You know I hated being the baby, and was really happy when she came along," I explain, pointing to Bonnie and trying to get mother to understand.

Stupid me, I had no idea what a little brat she was going to turn into. Doesn't Mom get it? I don't want attention.

"So how was your first day of high school?" Dad asks changing the subject,

I shrug, "Okay."

"That's all? How are your teachers?"

"Most of them are pretty nice."

"All except Miss Ditch." Annie chimes in.

"So who's this Miss Ditch?" Dad asks.

"My gym teacher," I say.

"And what's so bad about her?"

"Everything."

Annie knows just what to say, "Like in all our gym classes, she uses last names, and tomorrow, Kennie needs money for her gym suit."

I smile at her and sigh with relief.

"How much?" Dad asks. "Payday isn't until Friday. Annie, do you need money too?"

"Not until Thursday," she replies.

Well, we'll see what we can do for Kennie right after dinner. I can stop at the branch bank at the airport tomorrow to get what you need."

Bonnie bounces in her chair. Then she takes a spoon full of stew and swishes it in the air like an airplane coming in for a landing.

"How about you, Bonnie? Was school fun?"

"Yeah, I like Nursery school. It's great to have lots of kids to play with."

Mom is quiet, watching us, especially Bonnie. She reaches over and grabs Bonnie's glass of milk just in time. It was right in the flight path of the spoon-plane.

Disaster averted. Point for Mom!

When we all finish eating, Bonnie pushes her dirty dish at me, rather than taking it to the sink herself. No more arguments with her, I just slide it under mine, get up and take Dad's to the sink as well.

"Your turn to wash, so I'll clear the table and dry tonight," Annie says.

I run water into the sink and add soap powder from under the cabinet. It's neat how the suds seem to come out of nowhere. Not too many dishes tonight. Annie and I finish and hardly have time to say a word. I stand on my tiptoes to put the clean dry dishes up in the cupboard.

With no homework to do, we both head to the living room to watch "American Bandstand." Annie dances along while I tap my foot trying to keep time to the music.

But our fun is interrupted by Bonnie's fussing. "I don't wanna take a bath! I wanna watch TV with Kennie. It's not fair! She always gets to do whatever she wants!"

"Oh Mom, just stuff a potato in her mouth and put her to bed!" I mumble.

6. FIFTEEN DOLLARS

When Bonnie's fussing is over, I go to Dad's workshop, in the back of the basement, where he has a television set opened and parts scattered on the large wooden bench that he built himself. I disturb the sawdust on the cold concrete floor, and he looks up as he hears my footsteps.

"What brings my Minnie down to this cold corner of the castle?" he asks, grinning.

When he calls me by my special nickname, it's easier for me to remind him about the money I need for my gym suit. He pulls out his wallet and hands me the ten-dollar bill that's in it.

"Sorry, Minnie, that's all I've got. I can give you the rest after I stop at the bank tomorrow."

"Okay, Dad, thanks, but I need the whole fifteen dollars for tomorrow."

"Just tell your teacher that you'll bring in the rest on Thursday."

How can I tell Ditch this is all I've got? I can't tell her anything! Should I pretend I forgot? But then, I'll lose two points for not dressing and showering. And I need every point I can get in that class.

I run upstairs to find Annie.

"Annie, Annie! What will I do?"

"About what? Calm down and catch your breath. You look like you just ran a marathon."

"I need to pay for my stupid gym suit tomorrow and Dad only has ten dollars. Miss Ditch will be really mad at me, and I'll lose two points. With skills tests counting so much, I'll never pass PE!"

"Okay, I get the problem. You need five dollars by tomorrow. I have a few dollars, let's see."

Opening her purse, she finds two dollars and a quarter and gives it all to me.

"Thanks, but I need the rest for *tomorrow,*" I say, hearing the desperation in my voice.

"Just ask Mom," Annie says. "I'll even come with you."

We head to the kitchen where Mom is checking the fridge for dinner fixings for tomorrow.

"Hi girls, what do you need? A glass of milk?"

Annie turns and looks at me.

"Umm, no," I say.

"Well, then, what is it?"

"Oh, Annie," I say, losing my nerve. "You ask her."

"Ask me what?" Mom says. "Anything but 'can we move to Florida?' *again.*"

"No, that's not it," I say.

Mom looks at me puzzled. "Well, Kennie, I can't answer a question if you don't ask it."

Sensing Mom's impatience, Annie blurts out, "she needs money for her gym suit for tomorrow."

"Well, didn't she ask Dad?"

"Yes," says Annie. "But he didn't have enough, only ten dollars. I had a little, but she still needs $2.75."

"Okay, I'll see." Mom says and she goes to the front closet for her purse where she finds a little more.

"Thanks, Mom," I say, "but I still need almost a dollar more."

"Well, I guess you'll just have to raid the penny jar," she says.

It's either this, or face the Ditch and no points. I take the penny jar off the shelf, and count out sixty-five cents.

"How am I going to get all these coins to school without losing them?" I ask.

But before I finish the sentence, Annie is off to get an envelope for me.

I check again as I put the money in the crispy white envelope and seal it. Yay! That's it!

Annie smiles, closes the penny jar and puts it away. Then we both go brush our teeth and get ready for bed. I fall asleep quickly, knowing I have my fifteen dollars.

7. IN TROUBLE WITH MISS DITCH

Wednesday morning I wake up dreading gym class, the ugly gym suit, Miss Ditch and Mary Sue.

A knock on the bathroom door interrupts my thoughts. I open it and say good morning to Dad who's dressed in his old yard clothes, frumpy old trousers frayed at the bottom and an old shirt with the sleeves rolled up. He has just come in from working outside.

"Hi, Minnie, you're up bright and early. Looking forward to school today?"

"Not really. I have to face Miss Ditch and wear that stupid gym suit for almost an hour."

"The good thing about having gym first," he says, " is that it'll be over with and you can enjoy the rest of the day. You have some good classes too, right? Think of the chances you'll have to make some new friends."

"I guess," I say, not at all convinced.

#

Our neighbor, Jim comes bounding out of his house, just as the bus arrives. The three of us get on, find seats, and the bus starts moving.

Lost in my thoughts, I barely notice that the bus ride is over and we're at school already. I head for my locker and manage to get it open on the first try. This might be a good day after all. Let's see, I'll need my French, geometry, and history books. If I leave this English book here, will I have time to come back and get it before sixth period? Better not count on it. Four heavy books, gym shoes, money envelope and my purse, that does it.

Suddenly my locker door is slammed shut. I catch a glimpse of Mary Sue moving quickly toward homeroom, and I can hear her cackle above the noise in the hallway. I hope she's already sitting down when I get to homeroom so I can sit far away from her.

I guess it's not my lucky day. Mary Sue is milling around by the doorway acting all charming and nice with three boys gathered around her. I pretend not to notice and take a seat in the front row, next to Cathy. Then I open my French book and study the dialogue "*Bonjour, Jean, Comment vas-tu? …*" I read the passage over and over, until my mind can remember all the lines. I barely hear the bell ring or notice the Leprechaun standing right in front of me.

"Ah! Vous apprenez Francais, n'est-ce pas?" Mr. LeCourt asks.

"*Oui,*" I reply.

He talks about our Guidance Counselor appointments and calls our names as he hands each of us a card.

When he says my name, someone calls out "That's Pipsqueak Panic!"

I recognize Mary Sue's voice in an instant.

"*Pardonnez-moi?!*" The Leprechaun shouts in a voice louder than I thought he could muster. "That is unacceptable behavior and I won't tolerate it in my homeroom. Miss Parsonfield, this is your first and only warning. Next time you will report to the office and there will be consequences. Do you understand?"

The class is frozen in silence.

"Yeah…I mean, Yes, sir." She replies.

Whew, thank you, Mr. Leprechaun. I wonder if he was teased for being little in school too.

The bell rings and I gather up all my stuff, holding it tightly through the crowds that shove and shout. When I get to the locker room Mary Sue is right behind me. Miss Ditch greets us with a stern face at a table piled high with folded blue suits and a cash box just outside the locker room door. The coins jingle as I pull out the envelope with my money in it.

"What the heck is this, Panic?" she growls at me.

"It's my money for my gym suit," I try to speak loud enough so she won't make me repeat myself.

"You were supposed to bring fifteen DOLLARS." Miss Ditch bellows. "What's this, the contents of your piggy bank? I don't have time to count this now. Go to the end of the line, Panic."

Miss Ditch's mad face and the cackle behind me are almost unbearable. I bite my lip, trying not to cry, and let the other five girls get in front of me.

Parsonfield says, "thank you for the lovely outfit," in a sarcastic tone as she gets her gym suit and disappears into the locker room.

I sigh with relief that she's out of sight for the moment. The line moves up, another girl comes and I tell her to get in front of me.

"You sure are nice," she says sounding a bit puzzled.

But soon, I am face-to-face with Miss Ditch again. She grabs the envelope and rips it open, as two pennies go rolling on the table and onto the floor. I get down to pick them up, as much to retrieve the coins as to escape the sight of Miss Ditch's angry face. She proceeds to count my money down to every last penny. I want to tell her she can trust me. But I don't say a word as I add the last two pennies to her pile on the table. She had to count each coin one by one, just to make it take forever. Finally she puts the dollars into the coin box and slides the coins to the side of the table, pushes them into her other hand and adds them to the box, slamming it shut.

"Let's see, you need a small, probably an extra small suit would fit, but we didn't order any of those. Here, now hurry up and dress out."

Miss Ditch stomps into the locker room after me, and shouts, "As soon as you're dressed, grab a stick, get out to the field, we'll do our warm-ups, and then begin field hockey drills."

I change into the blue jumpsuit.

Yuck! These elastic bloomers are so uncomfortable. But no time to think about that now. I snap up the front of my suit, buckle the belt around my waist, and squeeze my feet into the old gym shoes. Ouch! They really pinch my toes. At least something about me is growing. The locker room is almost empty so I take the shortest hockey stick on the way out the door, and run to the field.

"It's about time you joined us, Panic!" Miss Ditch shouts at me.

Everyone is lined up for exercises. The girls look like rows of blue soldiers, standing at attention. I take a place in the last row. "Jumping jacks: 1, 2, 1, 2, 1, 2, 1, 2…" Ditch counts at the front. Everyone copies her movements. Then, it's down to do push ups. The grass is still damp and it feels awful, but we all follow her lead. Happy to get up again, we run in place, then around the track. I'm beginning to feel a bit better.

"Panic! How'd you get all the way up here?" Miss Ditch asks.

Uh oh. Just when I thought things were okay. What is she talking about?

"I'm just running on the track, Miss Ditch," I call out. "I don't really know what you mean."

"Panic! You are at the front of the pack. I'm just surprised, that's all," says Miss Ditch.

She then demonstrates the proper way to hold a hockey stick.

"Now step about four feet apart. We've got lots of room here. Nick you can give a ball to all the girls in your row."

As Nick hands out balls, Miss Ditch continues. "You will hit the ball to your partner directly across from you, and she'll stop it and pass it back."

Easy enough I think. Then I look up and see none other than Mary Sue directly across from me. Suddenly the ball is speeding right at me, like a huge bullet on the ground. I should jump out of the way, but instead I put my stick in its path. The stick jolts, the ball bounces over it and goes between my legs. Laughs and giggles surround me. I wish I could turn into a ladybug and disappear into the grass.

"Hey, Miss Ditch! I need a new partner!" yells Mary Sue. "Panic's a real Flunkie!"

Even Miss Ditch is laughing.

"Just give her a chance, Parsonfield. She's probably never played before. Have you Panic?"

Before Miss Ditch even gives me a chance to answer, she comes over and says, "part of the problem is this stick. It's got to be one of the biggest ones we've got. The top of it will be bruising your arms, which are almost as skinny as this stick. Could someone trade with her, please? The rest of you, get those balls moving through the grass."

Nick comes to my rescue and gives me her stick, I still have to choke up on it a bit to control it. Then I try to pass back to Mary Sue, but the ball curves to the side and heads directly for the girl next to her.

"Oh, jeez, why me?" Mary Sue says disgustedly.

After three more misses, I hit the ball exactly straight. Just as I begin to smile, I realize that it's only three-fourths of the way to Mary Sue.

"This is ridiculous!" she says, storming off the field.

"Panic, now what's the problem?" Ditch shouts looking at me.

"I'm trying, really I am, Miss Ditch." I answer.

"You're *trying* all right Panic, trying our patience. Okay, girls, it's time to head for the showers."

I sigh with relief and run as fast as I can with my stick in my hand. When I get there, I grab a towel, undress, put all my clothes in my locker, wrap the towel around myself and walk into the showers. Yikes, this is horrible! One huge yellow-tiled room with a dozen showerheads on each side, and a hook up high between them. I don't want anyone to see me naked. I notice the stalls and quickly make a dash for one, and close the door. Whew! I set my towel on the small shelf and turn on the water. It's freezing cold. I grab the soap bar, make some suds, teeth chattering, then rinse with cold water, dry off, wrap myself in the towel, and get out of here, before anyone catches me. No one knows who has her period when, but since I've never even had one, I'll have a harder time pretending. When I leave, another girls goes in. I come out and Miss Ditch gives me two checks in her little lined book. Those have got to be two of the hardest-earned checks anyone will ever get in this place.

Hurry, hurry, I keep telling myself. All set and with a minute or two to spare.

Mary Sue suddenly shows up and says, "Panic, don't you ever try to be my partner in here again! You got that, Pipsqueak?" Of course she's out of earshot of Miss Ditch.

Before I can think of a response, the bell rings. *Hallelujah*!

Now I've got to get all the way to geometry class. At least I know how to get there today. I feel frazzled, and my mousey blond hair is probably curling in all directions, but I survived. One gym class down and eighty-nine to go.

8. BULLIES IN THE BATHROOM

Soon it's time for lunch. Rushing to my locker, I toss my French and geometry books in it. Boy, do I have to use the bathroom badly! I look around for a friend—someone, anyone, so I don't have to go in there alone.

In desperation, I grab the arm of a girl heading to the cafeteria.

Startled, she jumps and says, "Hey! What are you doing?"

"Please," I say, in my small and squeaky voice, "*please* come into the girl's bathroom with me!"

She looks at me like I'm crazy. "Why?"

"Because I really need to go and there are some mean girls in there smoking."

"Well, I don't really have to go," she says, pulling away from me.

"Please," I beg her. "I need you to come with me. You can go into a stall and pretend. I don't want to get trapped by them."

"Well, all right. But just this once, and if there's any trouble, I'll book it outta there in a flash."

"Thanks a bunch," I say. "You're a real life saver."

I gingerly push the door open, just a crack, then almost halfway, and the smell of cigarette smoke comes pouring out. I head in with the other girl close behind.

"Hey, you!" one of the girls snarls at me.

"You told on us yesterday! You weren't out of here two minutes, and a teacher was in here yelling at us! You'll get your reward," the tall girl shouts pointing her finger at me. Like a ferocious dog, she lunges at me.

Then she sees the girl I begged to come in with me, and turns to her. I quickly slip under her arm and past the smokers while their attention is on the other girl. I make it into the stall, lock it quickly, and use the toilet. On the other side of the stall door, I hear bits of the ringleader's voice.

"…Makin' trouble for us… Okay just LEAVE."

I know they are out there waiting for me. I've never been so scared. There's no choice but to come out. Slowly I turn the latch. In an instant, I see several pairs of shoes gather in front of my stall.

I open the door, and now there's one more girl here—Mary Sue!

No chance for survival now. I am really dead.

Mary Sue sneers, "Well, well, if it isn't Panic the Pipsqueak. Somebody said you were smart. But they were wrong. Dead wrong!"

"Why'd you call her Panic?" the ringleader asks. "You know this one?"

"Yeah, Vicki. Her name's Panic. She's the dummy in my gym class who can't do anything right."

"That's for sure," says Vicki. "Yesterday she sent that big burly gym teacher, you know, Amazon Lady, in here and the teacher threatened to send us all to the office."

Turning to me, the leader grins, "We have a promise to keep. Remember?"

My throat is paralyzed; I can't utter a word.

"C'mon, you must have something to say for yourself," Vicki persists.

Mary Sue chimes in, "She doesn't speak up in gym class either. I wasn't here yesterday. What did you promise her?"

"A cigarette tattoo," Vicki tells her. "We just need to decide where we're going to put it."

I am sweating, trying hard not to cry, and unsure of how to defend myself.

Pulling together every bit of courage I can, I blurt out in a weak voice, "I didn't tell anyone anything yesterday. It's the truth."

"Oh yeah? So why did Amazon Lady show up within a minute after you left? Don't try to convince us that it was just coincidence."

Two girls grab my arms as my books spill to the floor. One starts to reach for my purse. "Okay, Vicki, we'll hold her; you do the damage."

"Wait a minute. Where do we leave our lovely mark? Her face? Neck? Arm? Leg? Hand? Butt? We want it noticeable, so people will know we mean business, but let's spare her ugly face this time."

"On her neck," says the puffy blonde. "We could make it look like a hickey." She giggles.

"Naaa, no one would believe it." Vicki says, "No boy would even talk to this little kid. Let's put it on her hand, like when they stamp your hand at the fair. What do y'all think?"

Mary Sue looks pleased. "Yeah, that sounds good."

They are holding me so tight, I can't struggle. When I try to scream, my throat lets out a tiny chirp. Vicki pulls out an opened pack of cigarettes from her purple purse, shakes the pack and takes the cigarette between her index and middle finger. Another girl pulls out a match and lights it. My whole body is trembling.

Vicki takes a few puffs and walks toward me, as Mary Sue holds my hand so tightly I think the bones are going to break.

The door crashes open, and a tall, muscular teacher stands in the doorway.

"What's going on here?" the teacher asks sternly. "The smoke is as thick as fog again. Didn't I see y'all in here yesterday?"

Everyone freezes. No one answers. Vicki scrambles into a stall, and we hear the john flush.

Amazon Lady steps to the doorway and blows her whistle. Four more teachers arrive. Amazon Lady has the smokers "escorted" to the office, but not Mary Sue. I guess the teacher didn't see her here yesterday. She lets me gather my books and purse, and tells me to go to lunch and to stay away from this crowd.

I certainly would if I didn't need to use the bathroom. But since we are not allowed to be in other hallways during our lunch period, this is the only bathroom I can use. I don't stay long enough to find out Mary Sue's fate. Right now, I really don't care.

I hurry into the lunchroom and look for a familiar face. At one table, the kids are all laughing and pointing at me. In the middle is the girl who came into the smoky bathroom with me. Quickly, I turn my head away, pretending I didn't see them. I find Sharon at the far table, and hurry over and ask if I can leave my books with her while I'm in line.

"Sure," she says, but notices how frazzled I am. "Kenda, what's the matter? You look awful! What happened? Wait. Go get your lunch and then come back and tell me," she says, sounding truly concerned.

I get in line, being careful not to look in the direction of the table that was pointing and laughing at me. When I get my tray I hurry over to sit by Sharon.

"Okay," she says leaning in towards me. "Spill."

"I almost got a cigarette tattoo." I gasp. "The Amazon Lady rescued me."

"What? Get a grip."

"Okay. You see yesterday I went in the bathroom across the hall by myself and there were some mean girls smoking in there. They threatened to give me a 'cigarette tattoo' if I told on them. But, I swear—I didn't."

"So you went back in there today, alone *again*? Oh, Kenda, are you asking for trouble?"

"Actually, I didn't go in there alone. I grabbed that girl over there and talked her into coming in with me," I explain.

"But, the head of that gang, Vicki, claimed I told on them, 'cause a teacher came in right after I left yesterday."

"But that was a coincidence, right?" Sharon asks.

"Yes. The teacher came in while I was still there today," I continue. "Then she blew her whistle and more teachers showed up."

"Oh yeah, we did hear a whistle," Sharon says. "But what are you going to do about it? You can't let them bully you like that."

I shake my head. "Beats me. If I tell anyone, those mean girls will *really* be out to get me!"

#

I actually make it on time to English class since I've learned to find holes in the crowds that fill the stairways and hallways. Maybe, Annie was right, things will get better.

My English teacher, Mrs. Anders steps out in the hallway when she sees me coming. "Your guidance counselor told me to let you know that I patrol the girl's bathroom on this hallway," she says. "There have been some problems in the one by the cafeteria." Her voice drops to a whisper. "So we are making an exception to the rule and giving you permission to use this one."

I smile at her and a feeling of enormous relief washes over me. Class passes quickly as we work with partners summarizing literary passages in our textbook.

When the bell finally rings, I grab all my stuff and race out the door. I run down the sidewalk to the first bus, anxious to get home. But, there in front of the steps, Vicki stands with her arms folded across her chest.

"Just where do you think you're going, Pipsqueak?" she says looking down at me.

The driver steps off the bus, and Vicki takes off.

"So, are you coming with me today, little one?" the bus driver asks me.

"Um, yeah, of course."

"Well what are you waiting for? Get on."

I climb the steps carefully and take the first empty seat I see.

Soon we are at our stop, and I get to talk to Annie.

"Well, things went a lot better today, I'll bet," Annie says, with a kind smile.

"Not really. Miss Ditch made me go to the end of the line so she could count every last penny in my envelope. No one else had to empty a penny bank to pay for a stupid, ugly gym suit. My field hockey stick was way too long and Mary Sue announced to the whole class that she didn't want to be my partner, 'cause I was such a flunky."

"Why did she say that?"

"Well, I just couldn't stop or return the hockey ball. You know I'm not athletic, but I don't act uncoordinated on purpose. She doesn't have to make such a big deal about it in class."

"Just ignore her."

"That's easy to say, but it's impossible."

"Then pretend to ignore her, and she'll give up picking on you sooner or later. She does it to get attention, and act like she's somebody. If she felt good about herself, she wouldn't have to make other people feel bad. The important thing is you can't let Mary Sue or anyone else intimidate you."

"Well the smokers won't be able to give me a hard time in the bathroom, anymore. When they were taken to the office, someone must have used my name and told my guidance counselor. My English teacher talked to me before class. She said I can use the girl's room by her classroom."

"It blows my mind how fast news travels in our school as big as it is," Annie says. "You're lucky to have people watching out for you, Kennie."

9. BULL'S-EYE

Field hockey is finally over. Thank goodness I got a ninety-eight on the written rules test, because I got a ZERO—yes a zero—on the skills test. Too bad she didn't give points for the bruises on my ankles and shins. They should have been worth something. I never figured out how to stop or hit that stupid hard ball to anyone. It's no surprise that I never got picked for a team, so I never actually *played* field hockey. But it doesn't matter now. Today, we start our unit on archery, which, thank goodness, doesn't involve picking teams.

I go to the locker room and get into my ugly blue suit.

It doesn't seem so awful anymore. Guess it makes us all feel part of something. I'm not sure what. But because we're all subjected to this humiliation, there's some odd form of camaraderie among us. And after four paychecks, I finally got new gym shoes. We go to the gym first for rules, safety reminders and exercises.

Miss Ditch explains, "There are six targets in the field. You will line up behind the bases. Only one person, the one on the base in each line has a bow and arrow. After my 'ready set go', release one arrow. After six arrows have reached the targets, you'll hear another 'Ready, set, go.' Release, wait until all arrows have been shot, and prepare the third time. When the whistle blows the scorekeeper will retrieve the arrows, write the scores on the sheet, bring the arrows back to the base, and pass the score sheet on to the next girl. We'll do this until all of you have had a turn to shoot three arrows."

Miss Ditch then demonstrates how to hold the bow, and insert the notch of the arrow into the string. Then she shows us the correct stance when pulling back on the string and releasing the arrow.

Miss Ditch continues with "as part of President Kennedy's physical fitness program, we'll be starting our coordination exercises. They are just like jumping jacks, but instead of two positions, there are four positions to the count of four. All right, let's get in rows for warm-ups."

"Follow me," Miss Ditch says, as she demonstrates the four positions.

We copy her like a bunch of monkeys. All the girls in front of me seem to be catching on. I can't keep up. A few girls around me start to giggle. Everyone is in step, but I am clueless. The harder I try, the more confused I get.

"Panic! Just what do you think you're doin' back there?" the thundering voice echoes through the gym.

Now everyone is laughing.

"Panic, if you can't follow, get up here and lead these exercises. At least then y'all will be facing the front."

I creep to the front of the gym with my head down, trying to ignore all the stares, trying to picture each position in my head as I go.

"Hurry it up, we haven't got all day," Miss Ditch says.

"All right, Panic. Now that you are up there, let's MOVE!"

I count unevenly and soon everyone is moving and laughing, with limbs in every direction

"Company HALT! That's enough. Panic! I can't believe such a simple 1, 2, 3, 4 can be turned into total chaos. Let's get out to the field." Miss Ditch looks in my direction and shakes her head.

Walking slowly I watch my feet as the dew gets my new sneakers wet. So much for my nice new gym shoes, at least they're not expensive Keds.

The loud sound of my name being yelled jolts me back to the immediate destination. I look up only to realize that the whole class is already in lines up on the far field, with the six targets in view in the distance. I break into a run, and soon get into the shortest line.

After many 'ready, set, gos', and faint thwump, thwump, thwump sounds, it seems like this is taking forever. Over and over I hear that commanding voice. Miss Ditch has the most amazing vocal chords. You'd think she would have worn them out by now, especially since she does this five times a day.

Finally, it's my turn. After the whistle, I run down to retrieve the arrows shot by Nick who was right in front of me; her scores were 5, 1 and 1. Sprinting back, I hand her the clipboard with her scores on it, take my place on the base, and set down two of the arrows. The other 5 girls are almost ready, so I find the notch on the arrow's stick and think about exactly how to stand, hold the bow, fit the notch on the string and wait for the 'ready, set, go'. The picture in my mind is totally clear. I raise the bow, check that my legs are apart and my elbows bent. Then, I place the arrow on the string.

"Ready, set, go!"

I pull the string back with all the strength in my right arm, close one eye and look down the shaft of the arrow with the other eye lining it up straight at the bull's-eye. Then I carefully move both arms up keeping them together as if the bow, arrow and arms are glued in this position. Keeping my eye on the target, I imagine the perfect arc for the arrow to travel. Yes, that's it. Release!

"*Thwump*!" my arrow hits the target, right in the center.

"Panic! That's amazing! A bull's-eye! This is your sport! Where did you learn to shoot an arrow?"

I am so surprised. I stammer, "Uh… Uh… Miss Ditch, that's the first arrow I ever shot."

The entire class is totally silent, staring at me. I glance at Parsonfield with her mouth hanging open. The rest of the class must be just as shocked as I am.

"Okay, girls," Miss Ditch shouts. "Get your second arrows!"

I pick mine up, and try to do exactly what I did the first time. The muscles in my arm hurt from the weight of the bow. Waiting for the others to get ready, my arm drifts downward by itself. By the time I hear the three words again, I have straightened my arm. At the sound of "go", I let the arrow fly. I hear the faint *thwump*, and a shooting pain starts in my elbow. The string is vibrating against my arm.

How can this be called a 'funny bone'? There is nothing funny about it. The sting travels all the way up my arm, and I want to scream, OUCH!

On my third arrow, I can barely lift my bow, but go through the motions as best I can. Just as Miss Ditch bellows out, "ready, set, go!" I pull back the string and release the arrow. It hits the ground about half way to the target. I am so glad I'm last. Maybe everyone will head back and not notice.

The shrill whistle blows and six girls run to the targets to retrieve the arrows and count the points.

I got ten points, but the pain is horrible. We all race back to the locker room. I'm one of the first to get there so I snatch a towel off the pile and slip into a shower stall. As I hold my wounded elbow under the spray, this is one time I'm glad the water is ice cold.

When I come out, Miss Ditch is there with grade book in hand, "Panic, today you gave me a glimmer of hope that you might be able to do something well in here."

"Thanks, Miss Ditch," I hear myself say as my mouth forms a faint smile.

10. GYMNASTICS

After two weeks my left elbow is finally better. The bruise on my elbow has gone from a purple grapefruit to a small greenish-yellow blur. The pain isn't so bad anymore, but the score on my archery skills test lives on as another zero in Miss Ditch's black grade book. Yes, black is the perfect color for it. Today we start gymnastics. Only time will tell if this is a good thing.

Miss Ditch blows her whistle. "All right, everybody in the gym!"

I finish snapping up the front of my suit and fixing the belt as I become part of the herd heading into the gym and forming lines. I still can't do those stupid coordination exercises. They are even worse than when we started, eight different positions to a count of eight. Miss Ditch has clearly given up on me—she just lets me make up my own and count to myself at the back of the gym. Since I'm not even in a row, I don't distract anyone else. Miss Ditch also has this idea that if I watch all the other kids, eventually I'll figure it out. For now, this feels like a comfortable truce.

"All right, that does it for warm-ups," says Miss Ditch. "Y'all come over to this side of the gym, and I'll explain what we'll be doing for our next unit on gymnastics. We'll start with the pommel horse. You see, it's pretty well padded, except for the two handles." She explains as she pats the top of the large, cylindrical *body*.

"The spring board in front helps give you momentum to get over the horse. I'll demonstrate."

Miss Ditch strides to the other end of the gym, runs, plants her two feet squarely on the jump board, and sails over the horse with one hand on the right handle, both feet off to the left, and toes pointed. Even with her short legs she makes it look easy, a combination of muscle and grace.

"All right, girls," she says once she's landed perfectly on the mat. "Line up in order of approximate ability. Nick, you start. Seven years of ballet should serve you well for this."

Miss Ditch walks down the line commenting: "Poison, move up about five. You should be pretty good at this. Norwell move up a few. Parsonfield, you can move up, in front of Norwell. Panic! What are you doing here? Go to the end of the line so you can observe as many students as possible."

"I only had three girls behind me." I mutter, knowing Ditch won't hear me above the usual chuckles and snickers.

"The idea is that you watch each person in front of you carefully, and think about exactly how she moves. This will help you when it's your turn. I'll be here by the horse to spot you. Okay, Nick, Go!"

Nick runs at a good pace across the gym, both feet land perfectly on the jump board and she flies over the horse as if her body is being controlled by some magical force.

"Wow! That was beautiful!" I whisper to Mason, the girl in front of me. Some girls are pretty good, and a few just barely make it over. Miss Ditch makes two girls go back and try it again. It's getting closer to my turn. I hope I can do this on the first try.

"Panic!" The sound of Miss Ditch's loud voice breaks my train of thought.

"Yes, Miss Ditch," I answer instinctively, as I look up. One of my classmates is sprawled on the floor in front of the horse.

Miss Ditch shouts at me, "I said, 'Girls Don't Panic!'"

Everyone looks at me and laughs. Then the girl on the floor shakes her head, her red ponytail hanging to one side. She leans on her arm and struggles to get both of her short, chubby legs under her body. Miss Ditch helps her up. She seems to be all right, just a little shaken and scared. Slowly, she makes her way to the side of the gym, rubbing her thigh.

Maybe Miss Ditch will forget about the last few of us.

"All right, Jones," Miss Ditch calls out. "You're next. Let's move it!"

So much for that happy thought of being forgotten.

The next girl runs, jumps and just clears the horse.

Next, the chunky body in front of me runs, jumps, grabs both handles and pulls up her legs just in time to get them over the horse.

"Well, you made it. But what were you supposed to be doing?" bellows Miss Ditch at my classmate.

"Umm…I thought my one hand couldn't hold me, so I decided to use two."

"I'll let it go this time, but that'll count against you on the skills test. Okay Panic, go!"

I tell myself to ignore all the eyes on me.

I start running, focused on the jump board ahead, knowing I need to plant both feet firmly on it, which is exactly what I do. Then what? Grab the handle with the right hand and let my body fly off to the left. Here goes. It works! My legs were actually soaring through the air! I made it over the horse!

"Panic! That wasn't bad," says Miss Ditch. "But what the heck did you do all that running for? You stopped on the board. A dead stop. The whole reason for getting a running start is to build up momentum so you are propelled over the horse. That way you don't have to work at getting over."

I am so relieved I actually made it that I really don't care about how and why.

"Miracles will never cease." Mary Sue's unmistakable voice carries through the gym. "Panic made it over the horse1"

She can say it, but I can choose to ignore her comment, which is exactly what I do.

11. REPORT CARDS

It's the tenth week of school and today our homeroom teacher passes out report cards for the first quarter.

"Nice job there" he tells one student.

"Well done."

"Looks like you could use some help in French, come in any day after school and I'll be happy to help you."

Finally he gets to me.

"Well, Kenda, it looks like you've got all the hard courses mastered. But what's this H & PE grade?"

Before I can answer, another teacher calls Mr. LeCourt to the door. Parsonfield glares at me. Then she grins, and snatches the card out of my hand.

"What? Ditch gave you a "C"? I can't believe it! Anyone else would have failed. She is so stupid in gym class, y'all just can't imagine," she announces to the entire homeroom while pointing at me.

I shrink down in my seat, wanting to explain that our grade isn't all skills test scores, wanting to ask for *her* report card, wanting to embarrass *her* in front of everyone. I scarcely hear anything else, the urge to smack Mary Sue across the face wells up inside me.

The bell rings, Mary Sue throws my report card on the floor, someone steps on it. I reach down and grab it. When I look at the smudged paper, I see not only the "C" at the top but four "A"s and a "B" in English. I smile. As I make my way to the gym with my suit, shoes, books and purse in hand, my mind wanders back to Dad talking about how my other classes must be better. I hope he's not going to be upset about a "C". Annie and I have always had all "A"s and "B"s on our report cards.

When I see Parsonfield in the locker room, I can't help but wonder why she always has to spoil my happy moments. Why does she hate me? Is she jealous of me?

As soon as we line up for exercises in the gym, Parsonfield gets in the front row.

"Miss Ditch, I can't believe you gave Panic a "C" in this class! What? Did you feel sorry for the poor clumsy pipsqueak?" Mary Sue asks with her hands on her hips.

"Young lady, you do not challenge a teacher like that, especially about someone else's grade, which is none of your business! Now get up here and lead these exercises."

Oh boy, Miss Ditch gave it to her. I go through motions of coordination exercises. I think I'm finally counting evenly since I change positions the same time everyone else does. Of course, my arms are up when theirs are out, and only rarely are my feet together when theirs are. Miss Ditch acts like she doesn't even notice. *It's fine. There are times when it's good to be invisible, and this is one of them.*

"Okay, girls, today we start basketball. We'll do drills all this week, then, if I think you're good enough, we'll pick teams and you can play. With two courts, the majority of you will be able to play. Those who aren't in the games will practice dribbling, passing and shooting with the extra hoop over by the locker room."

"Let's get started—make two lines. Here's how it's done," she explains as she bounces the ball. "Use your fingertips for better control. When you get to the other line, do a bounce pass like this." Miss Ditch sends the ball directly to Nick. Without missing a beat, Nick's right hand makes contact with the ball, and *bounce, bounce, bounce*… back across the gym she comes. When all the girls in the other line have basketballs, the dribbling sounds like a dozen big bass drummers.

A ball comes toward me. Instinctively, I grab it with both hands and bounce it across the gym being careful to use my fingertips. I feel like I can get the hang of this pretty easily.

After a few more rounds of dribbles, Miss Ditch blows her whistle. "Okay, there are five hoops, so get yourselves into five lines," she commands and passes a ball to the girl at the head of each line.

Holding the ball, Miss Ditch bends her knees, moves her arms upward starting at her waist, releases the ball in a perfect arc while keeping her eyes on the basket. *Swoosh*! In it goes without ever touching the backboard.

"Each of you will take a shot just like that," she says. "Pass the ball to the next person and keep rotating until I blow my whistle."

We practice, and on the third try, my ball hits the backboard in just the right spot and goes into the basket. I grin and want another turn while I still remember how I did it. But just as it's my turn again, the whistle blows.

In the next classes, we learn how to do lay-ups and more passes. We practice for a week and a half.

#

"Okay, let's play!" says Miss Ditch. "We have two courts, that means four teams. Nick, Norwell, Poison and Parsonfield. You have shown good skills, so you'll be the captains and play center. In turn, each of you will pick teammates, another center, two forwards and two guards. Nelson and North you can keep score. Patterson and Mason you'll be the timekeepers. "

The rest of us line up, hoping to get chosen each time a name is called. I quickly figure that four girls won't play since there are thirty-two of us. I think I'll be one of those four. Then it's last picks.

"Panic," Nick calls.

I jump, startled, and almost shout "Yay!" as I join her team.

The tallest girls are the guards, the centers are the most athletic, so I'm a forward, which means they expect me to shoot and score points. I have made a few baskets, so this could turn out okay.

As luck would have it, we're playing against Mary Sue's team. At the end of the first quarter, we are tied 14-14, the second quarter leaves us behind by two points.

"Panic, you've had the ball a few times. Don't be afraid to shoot. You can do it," Nick encourages me at half-time.

Nick and Parsonfield are center court for the toss up. Up, hit, over and the ball is coming straight to me on the court. I'm all alone. I reach up, catch it, face the hoop, bend my knees and spring up with my arms as I imagine the path of the ball. It moves perfectly in a smooth arc toward the basket, and I hold my breath. The ball swishes into the basket and I jump with excitement. A few girls gasp in amazement.

"Panic! You Idiot!" Miss Ditch hollers.

What? I want to scream. *Why did she call me an idiot?* My excitement dies. I look down at the floor, wishing I could just melt between the floorboards like the Wicked Witch in the Wizard of Oz.

"What basket are you supposed to be shooting for?" Miss Ditch's voice echoes.

"That still counts for us, doesn't it, Miss Ditch?" Nick asks.

Suddenly, I realize that we had switched sides of the court at halftime.

"No, it's in the other team's basket, so the points go to them." Miss Ditch says.

"Thanks Panic, not that we need your points, but we'll take 'em," says Parsonfield sarcastically as she puts her nose in the air.

I hang my head, my shoulders slump, and my knees feel weak. This must be how it feels to be stabbed when you're already dying. The rest of the game is a blur and we lose by two points.

#

At the dinner table, Dad says, "Hey Minnie, what are you thinking? You seem far away."

"I wish she was," Bonnie chimes in.

"Enough, Bonnie," says Dad. "Let's listen to Kenda for a change."

I glance around the table and sigh. "Oh, Dad, I want to quit school. I've had it. It's so totally embarrassing."

"So, we're talking about gym class again, eh?"

I nod. "I don't know which is worse, Miss Ditch, Mary Sue or my own stupidity."

"So what happened?" Dad asks.

"Nick actually picked me for her team and when I got the ball after halftime, I shot the most perfect basket! Then Miss Ditch called me an idiot for shooting at the wrong basket, and the points went to Mary Sue's team. We ended up losing. Nick, gave me a chance. And I blew it!"

"So why did Nick pick you in the first place?" Bonnie asks.

"She was just being nice, I guess," I reply, shrugging my shoulders.

Mom just shakes her head, takes off her glasses and wipes the lenses with her clean napkin.

"Minnie, this must seem like the end of the world to you now," Dad says. "But, there's a lesson here somewhere. Did you ever think about how funny that story is? Pretend it happened to some girl in a book—wouldn't you be laughing? There's something to be said for not taking ourselves too seriously, you know."

"I don't understand what you mean," I reply. "I just can't see myself saying 'Self, laugh. You are pretty funny,' in the depths of a disaster."

"Minnie, I predict that you will live to tell about this, and someday you'll be laughing."

Annie says, "Kennie, you are so good at everything else. You can't be serious about wanting to quit school over a dumb gym class. Just think, all you have to do is tough it out through one bad class every other day. And it's first period so you can get it over with early."

#

The next day, Mary Sue is waiting for me, blocking the doorway to our homeroom.

"Hey, where's your scarlet letter Panic? I don't see the big red "I" for Idiot!"

I look to the right, then quickly duck and slither under her left arm, in view of Mr. LeCourt.

Mary Sue whirls around just as I race to my seat.

I look at her through the corner of my eye. Her face is red; her fist is clenched.

Mr. LeCourt asks, "Mary Sue, is something wrong?"

"Nothin' I can't take care of later," she says, looking at me menacingly.

It seems as if the matter is dropped, but Mr. LeCourt gives me a nod as if he knows more than he's willing to let on.

When the bell rings to end homeroom, he follows me out the door and escorts me down the hall. But, Mary Sue has already run far ahead chasing after some guy.

I'm safe, for now, but the rest of the day I feel nervous, like I'm going to be jumped and taunted at every corner. But, luckily there are no more incidents the whole week.

I don't play in another basketball game. No matter who the captains are, I'm the only one who never gets picked for a team. I made one mistake and now I am discriminated against. It makes me angry that no one will give me another chance, even though I proved that I *can* score. Is there any hope that I'll be included in the next sport?

12. DECK TENNIS DISASTER

"Girls, the volleyballs we ordered haven't come in yet. So we'll be playing deck tennis instead. This game is also called ring tennis because it's played with this," Miss Ditch says holding up a thick rubber ring about the size of a dessert plate. The color matches our gym suits.

"Deck tennis was invented by Cleve Schaffer and was played on ships, as you might guess. It's not like tennis because you catch and throw the ring, rather than hit it. We'll play in teams just like volleyball, although it can be played as singles or doubles just like tennis. This ring is six inches in diameter and the original ones were made of manila rope. Ours is one inch thick rubber that is manufactured in Akron Ohio by Firestone," Miss Ditch continues.

I pay careful attention. This is the kind of trivia that she puts on our written tests.

Miss Ditch then paces the court along blue taped lines. "This goes twenty feet on each side from the net and the court is eighteen feet wide. Good news for Panic: this game doesn't require any specific skills, you simply throw and catch the ring."

A few girls chuckle. I try to avoid looking at Mary Sue even though she's right in front of me. But she turns around and stares at me with a big grin.

Miss Ditch continues, "The girl in the back right position serves to the opposite side of the court. If the ring lands on the floor or out of bounds, it's a point for the opposing team. Only the serving side scores. Teams rotate clockwise each time someone scores. Any questions?"

Silence follows.

"Okay," Miss Ditch says. "Since we have three courts, everyone can play. I'll point to the six captains, and you can pick your teams from over here." Miss Ditch motions to the side of the gym under the clock.

Just as I expected, I am the very last one chosen. But at least I get to play.

I'm the first on my team to serve, so I step back one foot in front of the other, holding the blue ring in my right hand. I swing my arm aiming toward the opposite half of the other team's side of the court. It flies over the net—*whoosh!* Cool! The girl on their team catches it, and sends it back over the net. Poison grabs it and returns the ring quickly. It hits the floor on the other side of the net. Point for our team. I serve again, and when it comes back, the girl next to me catches it, and throws it over the net again. When Parsonfield catches it she sends it to my side just on the edge of the court. It lands on the line. This counts as in-bounds, so we lose the serve, but it's 1 - 0 with our team in the lead.

Parsonfield's teammate serves. It comes straight at me. I catch it with my pinky. Then hold it and toss it back, over it goes. Two girls go for it and neither one grabs it, so the ring hits the floor.

"C'mon girls, you shoulda caught that, especially since Panic threw it. Now they get the serve again!" Parsonfield shouts.

"Rotate." Poison calls to us and I move into the front row. Oh No! I am directly opposite Parsonfield. She glares at me and snickers. A good serve by my teammate and now we're up by two points. She serves again. Back and forth, over the net the blue ring flies, again and again. Their team's toss lands out-of-bounds. So it's 3 – 0. Our team serves and over it goes. Parsonfield jumps up and grabs the ring, spiking it over the net in a flash. *Yikes!* It's heading straight for me! No time to get my hand up, the blue blur hits me hard in the face.

It feels like the front of my head has been cracked open. I look down to pick up the ring and see drops of blood on the floor. My fingers touch my wet cheek and I realize I'm covered with blood that's dripping down my chin and onto my gym suit.

"Miss Ditch, Panic's hurt!" one of my teammates screams. "She's bleeding."

I look up to see Parsonfield grinning through the net. The sight of her face makes me so angry, I want to scream. I try to go to the locker room, but my feet don't seem to move in the right direction. Mason comes and puts my arm over her shoulder to help me get to the wall. I sit on the floor and look down. My gym suit is more red than blue—yuck. Miss Ditch comes over with a bag of ice and a towel. She puts the ice on the side of my face and gets down next to me. Her face and the room slowly turn, even though I'm not moving my head.

"Panic!" she says. "Are you all right? How many fingers am I holding up?"

I look at her hand waggling in front of my face. "Three, I think. They'd be a lot easier to count if you'd keep them still," I say groggily.

"Does your head hurt?"

"Just a little," I put my hand up to my mouth, "But my tooth really hurts."

"Your tooth?" Miss Ditch asks.

"Yes," I say weakly, as I feel the blood still running out of my nose. The towel is getting soaked and I feel like I'm going to throw up.

I hate my life... I hate Mary Sue. She got the best of me again. I should have been watching the ring, and not her.

Miss Ditch blows her shrill whistle three times. Miss Walls the tall, brawny gym teacher appears out of nowhere with more ice. She and Miss Ditch put it behind my neck. By this time the whole class is gathered around, whispering.

Then I hear Nick's voice, "Is she going to be all right, Miss Ditch? Should someone go to the office?"

"Yes, Nick, you better get the nurse."

My neck and face are numb, and water is running down my back from the melting ice. It makes me shiver, and I wish everyone would just go away. The nurse comes and tells me I can get cleaned up in her office.

A couple of my teammates pull me up off the floor and put my arms around their shoulders as I try to walk between them. My feet are barely listening to my brain when I tell them to move. One step, then another; I drag my shoes along the floor.

"Well, if it isn't Kenda! Geez! Who tried to kill you?" asks George, a kid in my homeroom.

I don't even try to answer. It takes all my energy to move forward, sliding my feet along; they're too heavy to pick up. When I get to the nurse's office I lie down on a cot. The minute I put my head on the pillow, the nosebleed starts again. Quickly, the nurse props me up, and gets more ice and clean paper towels. When I sit up, I can tell the blood is trickling down my throat; it tastes yucky and makes me want to gag.

The bell rings. There's no way I want to go to geometry class looking like this, but I hate to miss math. I start to get up.

"Whoa, little Miss," says the nurse. "Don't even think about going to your next few classes. Can't take a chance of you passing out on the stairs and really getting hurt. You just sit quietly for a bit and when we're pretty sure you nose is done, we'll get you cleaned up. Do you feel dizzy?"

Not really. I was dizzy when I was little and playing in Mary Sue's yard. I remember the swing hitting me in the back of the head, the sky and the trees started spinning and then I saw nothing but bright yellow lines. Mom told me I had passed out. I feel sort of the same way, but I don't see the yellow lines this time. Instead of lying in the grass, I'm on a soft leathery cot. Instead of Mom standing over me, there's a nurse holding a clipboard. She asks me a lot of questions, but I barely answer her. I just want to collapse back onto the cot. Finally she lets me rest, with my head propped up on a few pillows. I drift off, not quite asleep, but not really awake either. A few other kids come and go.

The nurse hands me a warm wash cloth, and towel. I sit up enough to clean most of the blood off myself. It's caked up below my nose and dried on my gym suit. The nurse helps me change back into my blouse and skirt. Even my white sneakers have blood on them. She puts all my dirty clothes under cold water in the sink, wrings them out, and then puts them into a plastic bag. The bell rings, and I miss another class. I guess I don't need to worry about being excused.

"Are you getting hungry, Kenda?" the nurse asks.

"Not really," I reply. "I sure don't have enough energy to go all the way to the cafeteria."

Mrs. McNight gives me a package of crackers and a container of red jello.

"Try to eat this it'll make you feel better," she says. "And drink as much water as you can."

When the last bell of the day rings, the nurse asks me if I feel well enough to get to my bus.

"I think so," I say in a weak voice.

She makes a phone call, and soon Annie comes in.

Before I can ask why she's here, she rushes over and takes my hand. "What happened?" she asks, looking alarmed. "I heard all sorts of things. The Captain was worried that you didn't go to math class. I saw one of your friends outside the cafeteria and she said Mary Sue hit you in gym class."

"Yeah," I reply. "Mary Sue hit me in the face with the deck tennis ring. My nose wouldn't stop bleeding, and I've got an awful headache. Plus my tooth hurts and I'm so tired, I just want to go to sleep…" my voice trails off.

"Oh, Kennie, I'm here to help you get to the bus. Let's go," Annie says as she turns to thank the nurse. Mrs. McNight says a few words and hands her a paper.

We plod down the sidewalk and I hear a voice behind me.

"Look! It's Panic! She's still alive. We missed you at lunch!" a voice shouts.

I think it's Mary Sue, but I don't care. I just want to be home.

#

When we get to our stop, Annie gathers up my books and hers. I hold my bag of wet, bloody gym stuff and my purse. It's the longest walk home and I can barely make it up the hill, but I manage to drag myself to the cellar door as Annie gets out her key.

I am so tired that I dump my dirty gym stuff on top of the washer, crawl up the stairs, and go to the bathroom. In the mirror I see a pale, sad face with droopy hair and a bit of blood crusted under one nostril. I can't decide if I look worse or feel worse. There's only one thing to do. I take the ten steps to the room I share with Annie and plop down on my bed.

I don't remember anything until Dad taps me on the shoulder.

"Hey, Minnie, it sounds like you had a pretty rough day. Are you hungry or thirsty?"

"Huh? No not really," I tell him. "But my head hurts a lot. And this whole side of my face just aches."

"How about you just put your PJs on?" he suggests. "I'm sure you'll be more comfortable than in those school clothes. Just rest, and you'll feel better in the morning," he says as he pats me gently on the shoulder.

A few minutes later Bonnie comes bouncing in and jumps on Annie's bed.

"Ha Ha! You have to put your jammies on and go to bed before me," she says tauntingly.

"Please don't bug me. Can't you see, I'm in pain and just want to sleep?" I say.

"Oh. Sorry," Bonnie replies.

As I change clothes, Mom calls Bonnie to dinner. I put my head on the pillow and pull up the covers.

13. DR. PITT'S DRILL

I squint as I see the sunlight coming through the white curtains. Can it be morning already? My face hurts and feels like a blown-up balloon. Annie is gone. I just lie there not wanting to get up, afraid to look in the mirror. Soon Mom is standing in the doorway.

"Where is everyone?" I ask. "The house is quiet."

She comes over and sits on the edge of my bed, stroking my hair.

"Dad's off to work and Annie and Bonnie are at school. We thought it best to let you sleep, honey. But your face is swollen, and Dad said I should take you to the doctor. Would you like me to fix you some oatmeal?"

"Oh yes, with lots of cinnamon and a little sugar. I am kinda hungry."

I start to get up, and the room is spinning. I lean back on the bed.

"Mom! I'm dizzy and I need to go to the bathroom."

She comes back right away and helps me get up, first sitting, then waiting a bit and then standing. Okay I can do this. Holding her arm I make it to the hallway, where I put both my arms out to the sides to steady myself. When I get to the bathroom, I see the whole side of my face is swollen, not as big as the balloon like I thought, but it is puffy. Even my right eye looks more like an almond than an eye. Mom comes to check on me and makes sure I get back to bed all right. She fluffs my pillow and helps me get comfortable. A little later, she brings a tray with milk and warm oatmeal with cinnamon and sugar on top.

I eat and then think about what I'm missing in school. It's a health day and not a gym day. The one class I wouldn't mind missing.

When we finally get to the doctor's great big house and go inside the patient entrance we are greeted by his nurse, who smiles and doesn't even have to ask our names. She motions for us to come right into one of his patient rooms, and I'm glad that I don't have to go to the waiting room where people would surely stare and wonder what happened to me.

Dr. Caxton comes in; he sits on a stool and wheels it over to me. Gently he touches my forehead, and his warm hands glide down both sides of my face and my neck.

"So Kenda, what happened to this pretty face of yours?"

"I was hit by a deck tennis ring in gym class."

"Can you show me how big it was and exactly where it hit you?"

I hold my hands to form a circle with my thumbs and index fingers, and then move my hands to show where it hit me in the face.

"Hmm, with that kind of blow and since all the swelling is on one side, it's not likely to be allergy-related. Does your tooth hurt?"

"Yes! How did you know? "

"A trauma to this right front tooth would cause an abscess, which explains the fever, warm forehead, and the swelling. Let's get an antibiotic in you and you'll need to see your dentist right away to take care of the tooth," he explains as he scribbles on a small note pad, tears off the page and hands it to Mom.

"Be sure to get her to the dentist as soon as you can; otherwise the abscess won't drain, and the infection could spread."

"Thank you, Doctor. I'm so glad you were able to squeeze us in without an appointment."

"Not a problem at all. And you, Miss Kenda, watch out for flying objects, especially in gym class."

We stop at the desk for Mom to write a check and thank the nurse before leaving.

In the car, I stare straight ahead wondering how much this stupid accident is costing us, all because of Mary Sue. She should have to pay.

"As soon as we get home, I'll call Dr. Pasternak. Let's hope she can see you today, otherwise your father or I will have to take off from work tomorrow," Mom says.

I like Dr. Pasternak. We are the only kids I know who go to a lady dentist. She and her mother work together and speak with this wonderful accent. It's a little like my grandmother's. Dad said they are from Latvia, so I looked it up in the Encyclopedia, and it is pretty close to Poland and Germany.

On the way home we stop at the drugstore so Mom can get my prescription filled. She hands the paper to the pharmacist in the window. I wish we could eat at the soda fountain. But, I know Mom has had to spend too much money already, so I don't even ask. After she pays for the little bottle of pills and puts it in her purse, we get back in the car.

The ride home goes fast and I am hungry. I hope Mom is too, so that she can make us lunch right away.

#

We come in and hang our coats in the front closet. Mom reaches for the phone book and opens the cover to the numbers she calls often. She dials the numbers, and I am hoping that we can see Dr. Pasternak this afternoon.

"Oh, no… So how long will that be?... Both of them?.. Is there anyone else who could see her?.. Emergency? Well, sort of… No, not a car accident, but the doctor said she has an abscess and needs it drained right away. Okay, I'll just find someone close-by. Thank you."

Mom turns to me. "You are *really* out of luck, Kennie. The dentists are in Latvia for three weeks. It's not what they call an emergency, so the hospital isn't the place for you. I'll just have to find someone else to fix your tooth."

She turns the yellow pages in the back of the phone book.

"Hmm, d-e-n, here we are, dentists. This one is in McLean, about ten minutes away, let's try Doctor Pitt."

I don't even like the sound of his name. Mom dials the number and gets an appointment for tomorrow morning.

Well, there's one good thing about that... I'll miss gym class for sure.

"Dad will have to take you tomorrow. I'm behind at work. You know being the secretary in the logistics office at the CIA isn't easy, especially now when we are so busy with the inventory on top of our regular purchase orders."

Mom opens the fridge and takes out bologna and cheese to make us sandwiches. We sit on the green chairs to eat in our small dining room that barely fits a table and five chairs. As I pour some milk and take a pill, Mom and I have a rare chance to talk, just the two of us.

"Mom, how come you and Dad work so hard with jobs and this farm?" I ask. "In every other family we know, only the Dad goes to work."

"Kennie, you have to understand. Both your father and I know what it's like to be hungry. Even though we lived at the beach, it was the depression. My father left us and my mother worked what few hours they gave her as a hospital aide. Dad spent five years trying to escape Germany with his mother and little brother after your Grandpa left to find work in America. They had little more than the clothes on their backs. When they finally got to New York, your Grandpa still didn't have a job."

"So that was a long time ago and things are different now," I reply.

Mom continues to explain. "But once you've known what it's like to starve, you'll do anything to be sure your family never has to go though that. No matter what the government does, you'll never go hungry if you're self-sufficient. You kids are lucky, your Dad takes his responsibility as a father seriously and has worked so hard to be able to buy this little farm. We love you girls."

"I guess I'm always thinking about all the chores I have to do, and the roller-skating parties and movies I'm missing. It'll be a little easier now, knowing that you and Dad love us enough to be sure we have a good life no matter what happens in the world."

Mom smiles and says, "you know it's good for us to talk. I wish we could continue our conversation, but I have to go get Dad at work and Bonnie at school."

After Mom leaves, the house is quiet; it's really nice not having Hurricane Bonnie around. I turn on the TV, but there's nothing to watch except soap operas, 'Another World' and 'General Hospital'. You have to watch these shows every day to figure out who's related to whom and to make any sense of what's going on. It takes forever for anything to actually happen. How boring!

I wander downstairs and pick up the World Atlas, wishing I could bring Dr. Pasternak all the way back from Latvia. *The Iliad* is on my desk. I am such a slow reader, it'll be good for me to try to get ahead for English class. Surely, I'll have a lot to make up next week in school. I read until my eyes hurt.

I rustle through stuff in the bottom drawer of my desk and pull out the sketchbook I made from pieces of plain white paper stapled together at the top. I smile at the strange assortment of cartoon characters: Dick Tracy, Li'l Abner, Daisy Mae, Snoopy, the round-faced kids in Family Circus, Donald and Daisy Duck, and so many more marching across the pages. The last one is Joe Btfsplk, the scrawny guy in Li'l Abner with the black cloud over his head. I draw a Josephine Btfsplk with her own black cloud. She frowns and looks down. Sometimes I think I know just how she feels.

"Hi, Kennie! Are you feeling any better? Did you see Dr. Caxton? Are you going to be able to go to school tomorrow? Mr. LeCourt asked about you and so did the Captain," Annie blurts out the minute she sees me.

Then she stops and looks over my shoulder. "Wow!" she says, "those cartoons are really good!"

"Drawing makes me feel better. My tooth has an infection and Dr. Caxton says I have to go to the dentist to get it drained. And Dr. Pasternak is in Latvia! So tomorrow morning I have to go to some guy dentist we've never seen before, a Dr. Pitt."

She smiles and says, "I hope he's more pleasant than his name. But you'll be fine, you are the bravest."

#

Friday morning I wake up wondering if I heard Mom and Dad arguing last night about how much this was costing and who would take me to the dentist and how it wasn't really my fault or if that was just a bad dream.

Still I worry. We don't have money for all this tooth trouble. On top of that, Annie and I have never gone to anyone but Dr. Pasternak or her mother; why do they both have to be on the other end of the earth, when I need them here now? I wonder what this dentist will do; how do you drain an abscess? I don't even know what an abscess is!

I get up and look in the mirror hoping that my mouth will be back to normal, but it's still all puffy under my nose and up the side of my cheek. My eye is open a little more than yesterday.

"Kennie, how are you doing this morning?" Mom asks as she pokes her head in the doorway.

As I stand up, still wearing my PJs, she continues, "Dad will take you to the dentist this morning, but you need to get ready so he can go straight there after dropping me off at work."

I go back to my room and decide to wear a pretty dress, since I don't have to go to school. Lucky me, look at all the nice hand-me-downs from my cousin in New York. I pick a blue dress with small polka dots and a ruffle at the hem.

My bowl of cheerios isn't very tasty or maybe I'm just not hungry. Oatmeal always tastes better, but there's no time to cook it. After I brush my teeth and fix my hair, we all get in our sandalwood tan Ford Fairlane, except for Annie who is walking to the bus stop already. I'd much rather be with her and going to school than leaving for the dentist.

Dad drives Bonnie to her school first.

As she jumps out of the car, she asks, "how come Kennie doesn't have to go to school today and I do?"

She doesn't even wait for an answer as she races for the playground.

Mom shouts "Bye." Bonnie doesn't even hear her, or pretends she doesn't.

We drive to the huge modern building where Mom works. Mom pulls out her mirror from her purse and checks her bright red lipstick, Revlon's Cherries in the Snow.

The car slows to a stop. When Mom gets out of the car, the seams in the back of her stockings show below her brown and blue dress.

"Good-bye and good luck," she says, waving to me.

After she leaves, Dad is quiet. That's not good. Dad always likes to talk with me in the car unless he's worried or upset. I don't know what to say. I wish Annie was here. I look at all the buildings and trees along the way. We pass the McDonalds, Allyn's Men's Shop and Pat's Dress Shop. There's a school bus behind us.

Part of me wishes this ride would last forever and part of me just wants this whole thing to be over and done with. Soon, we pull into a parking lot of a two story medical building. I see the sign McLean Dental Office. I grit my teeth and clench my fists. We're here. Dad gets out and brings the newspaper.

"Come on, Minnie. Let's go. We need to deal with this tooth. You are going to be okay."

We walk next to each other and Dad pulls open the large wooden door, he waves his arm for me to go in. Inside there's a lady dressed in a black suit with black-rimmed glasses behind a desk. She sits with perfect posture, as if balancing an invisible book on her head.

"Hello. You must be the girl who had the bad accident in gym class. Have you ever been here before?"

"Umm, no."

"Then you'll have to fill out these papers," she says handing Dad a clipboard and a pen.

He takes the clipboard and sits down. I sit next to him in a cold leather chair. As he writes on the lines, I watch his pen make even strokes in a combination of script and printing. Every letter sits on the line like a row of birds on an electric wire. My stomach is doing flips and my hands are clammy. I don't want to be here.

Dad hands the clipboard back to the lady in the black suit. She nods, saying nothing. She's not even smiling. As I look around the room, the lamp is a miniature suit of armor. Dad and I are the only ones in the waiting room. This place gives me the creeps. Just when I am about to tell Dad that we need to split this scene, a lady in a starched white uniform comes through a door behind the receptionist.

"Kenda?"

I stand up slowly and turn my head back towards Dad. He starts to come too. The lady in white walks and speaks as stiffly as her uniform.

"You can wait here, Sir. She won't be long. Follow me, Miss."

As I glance back at Dad; he is unfolding the newspaper. The starchy-dressed lady escorts me down a long hallway and into a small room with a large black chair and white walls. She clips a paper bib on me and disappears.

Sitting in that huge, cold black chair, I feel like a dwarf in a giant's land where colors have been washed away. I start to calm down. I'm lost in my imaginary world when the door opens with a creak. In walks a tall thin man stroking his black, well-trimmed beard that comes to a point.

Reading from the clipboard on the counter, his deep voice with a slight accent says, "So what have we here? Hmm, looks like we have to drain the abscess and then do a root canal on number eight. This happened two days ago, so it's dead and we won't need novocaine."

Then he starts drilling. Annie always says I'm the bravest. I'm trying to live up to her words. The stabbing pain is so bad that I feel tears forming in my eyes. I am drooling all over the white paper bib, and I feel a tear roll down my cheek. The shrill drilling goes on. My hands grip the black leather arms of the chair so tightly I feel every tense muscle in them. If I were a spy being tortured this way, I'd tell every secret I knew in a second. The tears are forming little rivers down my cheeks now. The black-bearded driller is working like a robot and seems not to notice. Whirr, whirr, whirr…on and on for what seems like forever.

"Okay, almost done now." He says as the drill speed slows, and then stops.

I see the starchy lady behind me. I wonder if she was here all the time. She hands him two tiny white toothpicks, which he sticks up into the hole in the tooth and moves them up and down. They are wet and taste really strange, almost like a spice we add to pumpkin pie. Then I'm aware that the whole room smells like the same spice. After he takes out the miniature toothpicks, he takes a silver poker smaller than a pencil with a blob of white stuff on the end from the starchy lady. I feel the white stuff being pushed into the hole and the scraping of the end of the tool on the back of my tooth.

"Okay, Miss, that does it for today. Don't eat or drink anything for 30 minutes, and I'll see you again in a week to 10 days."

I can't believe that I survived that torture. As I stand up I see the indentations from my hands on the chair arms. The lady in white walks me to the end of the hall and I grab the doorknob to let myself back into the waiting room. As I open the door, Dad folds the newspaper and starts to get up.

"You need to make another appointment with the receptionist. Bye now," and the white lady disappears.

I can't believe that I have to come back here again for more torture.

Dad talks to the lady behind the desk, takes a small card from her and writes a check.

I bolt for the door as soon as he says his customary, polite "thank you."

"Looks like you've been through some ordeal," he says compassionately.

"It was horrible, a lot worse than almost drowning. It seemed like I was being tortured for hours. And to think I have to go back again. Dad that tooth is not dead!"

"Minnie, I think a special treat is in order this payday for a very brave girl. Now I have to get you home and myself to work."

"I want to go to school. I'm okay now."

"I don't think so, Minnie. I need to give you another antibiotic pill and some aspirin. Mom has already arranged for Aunt Helen to come over for a few hours this afternoon."

Groovy! A visit from Aunt Helen is definitely better than going to school.

14. MY FIRST JOB

It's Monday already. As soon as I get up, I dash for the mirror. Whew, my face is its usual pale self, no more swelling, my hair is a mess of mousy brown tangles, but that can be fixed… a lot easier than my tooth. I wish I could pretend that last week's accident never happened. I wish I could be someone else.

As I'm waiting for my turn to use the bathroom, Dad comes down the hall.

"Hey, Minnie, you're looking much better. How do you feel?"

"Pretty good, but I don't want to go to school. I *really* don't want to go to school. I'm dreading all the questions from teachers and the other kids, especially Mary Sue. I know she's gonna make a big deal about this whole thing and make the class laugh at me. I think Miss Ditch really likes her too. She always picks Mary Sue for a team captain and makes her look good at whatever we're doing in gym. That teacher hates me. Miss Ditch makes fun of me and the whole class is always laughing at me."

"Minnie, every part of your life can't be perfect. Did it ever occur to you that sometimes you *are* pretty funny? Try pretending you are a ladybug on the windowsill watching yourself. You just might laugh, too."

Mom comes out of the bathroom, and I go in quickly, thinking about what Dad just said. Nobody understands what it's like to be me! He should trade places with me for just one day. Then he'd know how stupid I feel! He'd know how mean Miss Ditch is and the humiliation of Mary Sue's comments. I grit my teeth and clench my fists, pretending to punch Mary Sue in the face.

I get in the shower and feel the nice hot water wash over me. "Relax and be calm," an inside voice says. Then, in my mind's eye, I see myself trying to do those coordination exercises, and I have to laugh. Maybe Dad's right.

After a quiet walk down the road and the usual ride to school, the bus pulls up in front of Page High. Kids pile out like it's just another Monday. I pick up my books and purse.

Pretending I'm a ladybug on the window, I see myself: a little skinny girl moving in slow motion. I wonder if I hid in the back between the seats, could I ride the bus all day? That wouldn't work. I'd never survive without lunch. But facing Parsonfield and Ditch is worse than no lunch. Maybe I could get off the bus and run away, but where?

"Hey, are you getting off or not?" The bus driver startles me.

I walk quickly down the aisle and step cautiously down the steps and onto the sidewalk. I look in both directions expecting Mary Sue to be standing there waiting for me. I hold my breath at every turn as I go to homeroom.

Nick rushes up to me in the hallway. "We missed you last week," she says. "Are you all right?"

"I'm fine now, but it was pretty awful. It's nice of you to ask."

"Yeah, we missed you." The unmistakable voice of Parsonfield chimes in as the three of us walk into homeroom together.

"*Bon Matin!*" Mr. LeCourt's cheery voice says as he looks at me. "I hope you are doing better, Kenda. We're glad to have you back. I have a pass for you to see your guidance counselor today. Mrs. Vankowski has something to talk with you about."

I take the pass and wonder why I have to see her.

Mr. LeCourt says, "No need for that furrowed brow. It's good, so don't worry."

"Thank you," I say as I take the yellow pass. "I'm fine now, but I'm sure I have a lot of make-up work to do."

"You are a smart cookie. You'll be caught up in no time, and if you need help in French, I'm here every day after school," the Leprechaun says with his feet moving as if doing a jig in the front of the room.

"Hey, Mr. L. can I ask you a question?" Mary Sue asks.

"Sure."

"How come you're *always* so happy, especially in the morning?"

"I love what I do. The energy of young people with genuine personalities and dreams makes everyday exciting, even with its crises that seem huge at the time. It beats teaching a lot of stuffy, rich old ladies at the Berlitz School of Languages."

"You mean you really *like* us?" Mary Sue asks, looking at him as if he just sprouted elf ears, "I thought teachers got paid peanuts."

"Yes, I really like you all, and I did take quite a pay cut to come here. But you have to decide what's important to you in life. Someday you'll understand."

When the bell rings, Nick, Mary Sue and I head for health class.

I am so dreading this. The last person I want to see is Miss Ditch. Why couldn't my guidance appointment be during first period instead of second? I let the others go into the classroom first, hoping Miss Ditch won't see me. If I could make one wish, it would be to have the power to become invisible.

"Well, look who's back! It's good to see you looking normal, Panic. I can't remember when I've seen so much blood except in a horror movie." Miss Ditch's loud voice has all eyes on me.

So much for that magical power of invisibility. I feel that I have to say something. I think and muster my courage.

"Miss Ditch, it was awful and painful, but it's all over."

Did I catch a glimpse of sympathy on her face, or was it my imagination?

"Do you want to talk about it?" she asks.

"Talk about it? Oh, no. Y'all saw it happen, so there's nothing to tell."

"Okay," she says. "Let's move on with roll call."

All through class my mind is wondering why Miss Ditch would think I'd want to talk about the blue ring Parsonfield heaved over the net and into my face. Does she expect me to explain why I didn't catch it or why I didn't see it coming?

When the bell rings, I can't tell you anything about the first aid lesson. I should have been paying attention.

#

Walking down the hall to my guidance counselor's office, I wonder why I was called there. Mr. LeCourt said that it was good. Did it have something to do with being out of school last week? Oops, I almost trip on the last step. I'd better watch where I'm going. I feel queasy as I turn the door knob to the guidance office. *Calm down*, I tell myself, *Mrs. Vankkowski is nice, and you know this is something good.*

The assistant smiles and says, "Good Morning! You must be Kenda. You can go right in. Mrs. Vankowski is waiting for you." She moves her right arm in a slow arc and points in the direction of the counselor's office.

I walk over to where the door is part-way open.

"Come in and have a seat, Kenda," my guidance counselor says in a friendly voice.

I pull my pleated skirt under me as I sit down and put my purse on the floor.

"Hello, Mrs. Vankowski," I say and try to smile even though I'm nervous.

"Well, Kenda, I guess you are wondering why you are here. Actually there are two reasons. I understand from Miss Ditch that you had a bad accident in her class last week. It's my job to follow up on incidents like that. First of all, it looks like you came through it just fine. But I'm sure it was no fun. Would you like to tell me about it?"

"No."

"I certainly won't ask you to talk about it if you don't want to. But sometimes talking about bad events can help make you feel better."

As I shake my head from side to side, Mrs. Vankowski continues. "Now the second reason I want to see you is because I have gotten an unusual request from a parent, and I thought you might be the perfect person to help me. You see, one of my students is having a hard time academically and needs to pass algebra in order to get into our vocational training program called Distributive Education. Her father called me and asked if I could arrange a tutor. Some difficult circumstances left the family without much money, so he can only afford to pay one dollar an hour, and I just can't ask a teacher to do it. I know you could, if you have the time after school and take the late bus home. Would you like to be a math tutor?"

I am so surprised. "Yes," I blurt out, "I'll do it."

"Great," Mrs. Vankowski says, "I hadn't expected that much enthusiasm. Mr. LeCourt will let you use his room, since he is always there for an hour after school and doesn't sponsor any clubs. Can you start on Wednesday?"

"That will be good," I answer.

"It's all set then. I'll let the others involved know that you'll do the tutoring. Thank you, Kenda."

After I leave, I realize that I was so excited I never asked the girl's name. I probably don't know her anyway. Out of nearly two thousand students in this school, I only know about 100 kids.

As I enter the classroom, the Captain studies my face.

"Well, Kenda, how was your meeting with Mrs. Vankowski?

I walk over to his desk so I can answer him without the whole class listening.

"I was surprised," I tell him. "I never thought I would be asked if I want a tutoring job."

"So? That means you are going to do it?"

"Yes. But I'm a little scared. What if this student doesn't do any better with my help?"

"Kenda, it's a big responsibility, and I'm glad that you are taking it seriously. You'll do just fine," the Captain reassures me.

The rest of the morning passes quickly and it's lunchtime. Since I got permission to use the upstairs bathroom, I even have time to go to my locker. I still see all the freshmen in the cafeteria, including the leader of the smoking gang and Parsonfield. I get my lunch, avoiding their table and go to the far side and sit by some girls in my history class.

Erik, the tall skinny kid in my homeroom, squints through his thick glasses as he maneuvers his way through the crowd of kids standing and chatting. He sets his tray on the table next to Norwell. I'm hoping she'll be nice and not act like most of the other kids, but she gets up and moves to another table without saying a word. Erik steps cautiously to our side and sets his tray between Sally and me. He never says much, and we know him only from homeroom.

"Hi," Sally says. "How are you doing?"

He looks pleasantly surprised, sits down and answers "Just fine, thank you."

His smile shows a row of very crooked teeth, the two in the front come together in a point. He uses his knife to cut his meatloaf into small, neat rectangles, and proceeds to stack them like blocks on his plate. Erik takes a bite or two of potato and chews as if he needs to think about every bite. I try not to stare and want to say something nice to him, but I'm afraid to interrupt his concentration.

Sally asks, "Erik, what are you doing?"

Erik leans back, crosses his arms, smiles, and mumbles, "I think I just proved that you can build a curved wall."

We all look at his "meatloaf wall" shaped like a "C".

"Groovy! Who would have ever thought of that!" Sally exclaims.

Erik beams and then gobbles up his meatloaf, brick by brick.

Sally looks at me. "Kenda, we've missed you in homeroom and history class. Would you like to borrow my notes?"

"Kenda, I know you missed school last week, too," Erik says, before I can answer Sally.

"I was out, and it was pretty bad, but I'm okay now. And yes, Sally, I would like to borrow those history notes. So much of the tests are about what he says in class."

15. A CLOSE ENCOUNTER

"Hah, so you've got a boyfriend." Vicki accuses me, as I put down my empty tray. "We saw you sitting next to Erik at lunch!" The whole gang is behind her ready to pounce on me.

"Yeah, he's not exactly Mr. Handsome, is he?" the one with the dyed blonde hair adds, and "by the way, we've missed you."

"Yeah, I'm sure," I mutter trying to be polite, but not really wanting to have a conversation with them.

"That's not what I'm talkin' about. We haven't seen you in the girls room in quite awhile. Have you learned to stretch your bladder so you don't have to pee in school anymore?"

Oh, get me out of here.

I squeeze around two other kids and make my way into the crowd.

This is one time when it's good to be small, I think to myself as I duck around the other side. Phew! Escaped!

A hand grabs the collar of my blouse.

"Not so fast, Pipsqueak! When I ask you a question, I expect an answer." Vicki, snarls in my ear.

"Umm…I don't have anything to say."

She's pulling tighter on my collar, I feel like I'm choking.

"Look, Pipsqueak, don't mess with me. You ought to know better. Now why haven't you been to the john? According to school rules, you're not allowed in any other hallways during lunch. And a goodie-two-shoes like you wouldn't break any rules now, would you?" Vicki growls at me in her raspy voice.

She continues, "remember, we still owe you a tattoo and I haven't been able to give it to you yet. You thought we'd forget! Not a chance, kiddo."

I feel my face turning bright red, I gasp for a breath, and she still has a hard grip on me. Suddenly she lets go and her feet fly out from under her. As I break away, I catch a glimpse of Erik behind her.

Did he manage to trip her? No time to stop and look. Gotta get out of here.

I slip through the crowd of bodies in the hall and head for art class. When I race in the door, the teacher's head pops up from his easel.

"Whoa! What or who is chasing you? The devil himself?"

"Umm, no, Sir."

"Say, Kenda, are you all right?"

"Yes, why?"

"Your face is flushed and you seem winded. Do you need to go to the nurse?"

"Oh no! I spent most of the day there last Wednesday. The nurse is nice, but I'd rather be in class. I'm all right."

Art class goes by quickly.

When I get to English, my last class, Mrs. Anders greets me with a smile. I am tired and don't really want to think about Jane Eyre. My mind drifts to Vicki, the smoking queen; I wonder if she'll be waiting for me when I leave the building this afternoon. If I go out the door by the library rather than the front door, I might be able to make it to the bus without her even seeing me.

When the bell rings, I hurry to my locker, head down the side stairs and out the door. Glancing around the library section of the building, I see the whole smoking gang standing by the sidewalk facing the front door. I make a dash to the bus and get on without being seen by any of them. Just to be safe, I sit on the side of the bus opposite from the building and sigh with relief. I survived another day. I can't help but wonder why, how, who or what made Vicki fall when she was ready to strangle me. Did Erik trip her or was it just a coincidence that he was nearby?

#

As Annie and I walk up the long dirt road to the house, she asks "Kennie, can you pick up the pace a bit? I'm anxious to get home; Karen's going to call me about the school play and I have tons of homework."

"Oh, sorry. It's just that I'm so tired."

"Yeah, I know it was your first day back and all. I guess everyone was asking about your ordeal last week. Did anything else happen?"

"The good thing is that I went down to see Mrs. Vankowski this morning and they want *me* to tutor a girl after school! I'll even get paid a whole dollar an hour! It's a lot more than we can get for baby-sitting!"

"Wow! That's pretty neat! Who are you tutoring?"

"I have no idea, some girl. I just hope I remember everything and that she's nice."

"You don't have to worry; you're so smart, it'll only take you a minute to re-learn anything you forgot."

We walk along quietly for a few minutes. Then I tell Annie about my encounter with Vicki.

"Annie, you remember the mean kids who smoke? You know, Mary Sue hangs out with them and Vicki, the Smoking Queen. That's what I call her…not to her face of course! Well, the weirdest thing happened when I took my tray back after eating lunch with Sally and Eric."

"Wait a minute, you ate lunch with a boy? That's got to be a first."

"Eating lunch with Erik is different. Most of the kids are so mean to him that they get up and leave the table when he tries to sit down near them and they call him "Retard." But Sally and I don't mind. I feel kinda sorry for him, 'cause you know it's not his fault."

"Okay, I didn't mean to interrupt; go on with your story. What happened with Vicki and Mary Sue?"

Annie hears the whole story, and I'm breathless by the time we get to the top of the hill.

"Please don't tell Mom and Dad about all this, especially at the dinner table! I don't want them to know about how much

Vicki is out to get me. I know how to avoid her, and I will tell a teacher if it's gets too bad."

16. TUTORING

The last bell of the day rings, and I go to Mr. LeCourt's room, excited to meet my tutee. When I get there, only Mr.LeCourt is in the room, and of course, he greets me with a smile and a cheery "*Bon après-midi.*"

I smile back and thank him for the use of his room.

"Not a problem at all. I'm here after school anyway," he reassures me.

A short red-haired girl walks in and says "I'm here for tutoring."

I jump up, excited to meet her.

But then Mr. LeCourt says "Ah, Colleen! Glad you could come today to catch up on the French you missed!"

I look at Colleen, puzzled. "You're not here for math tutoring?"

Mr. LeCourt chuckles, "we have two tutoring sessions going on today. Colleen is here for help with her French."

Just as I begin to wonder where my tutee is, in walks Mary Sue Parsonfield. She freezes after taking two steps into the doorway.

"You've got to be kidding me! *You* are my math tutor? I was expecting some cute guy."

I want to scream right back at her: *"You've got to be kidding me!" Oh no! What have I gotten myself into?*

Before I can say anything, Mr. LeCourt says, "Mary Sue, you know, Kenda is probably the best person in this whole school to help you in math. She's good at it because she's patient and sticks to it. We think that all you need is some time away from the boyfriends and the clique to really concentrate on the math. With a little help, you'll see you can do this."

Oh man, I sure hope he's right.

I turn to Mary Sue who is glaring at Mr. LeCourt. "We really should get started. When's your next test? Do you have your homework? Where are you in your text book?"

"Not so fast, Pipsqueak! This isn't the inquisition. You gotta understand. I haven't done homework in weeks. I just don't get this stuff. We're supposed to be on page 142, I'm on page 2. I have a consistent grade for the first terms: all 'F's. If you're gonna be my tutor, you gotta realize two things. One: you better be a miracle worker, like Helen Keller's tutor, and Two: I *don't* want to be like *you*. Got that?"

"Umm, yes. Look, I'm just as surprised as you that we are working together," I say, trying not to let my anger show at the people who set us up.

"Who said we're working together?" she challenges.

"I mean, we're both going to have to work at teaching you enough math so that you get your grade up. I don't think it's going to be easy. But you *need* to pass, and I've got the job of helping you. This is going to seem like torture to both of us, but it's just for an hour a day, until you get the hang of it."

"Correction! It ain't torture to you. This stuff is easy for you."

"Okay, whatever you think. But it's only easy 'cause I work at it and sometimes spend an hour or two on my math homework."

"I told you, I don't want to be like you!" Mary Sue says as she pounds her fist on the desk.

"Okay, okay. You only have to *really* try for this one hour. We better stop arguing or the hour will be gone and we'll have accomplished nothing," I say.

"All right, Mary Sue, let's sit down. When is this test?"

"Next Friday…a week from tomorrow. I don't even want to think about it. I know I'll flunk."

"Okay, then, what's your homework for tonight?"

She opens her book to page 142, and has pencil checks next to six problems. I sit down next to her and read problem 1 out loud. "If $x + y = 32$, and $x = 4$, solve for y."

That's pretty easy, I think.

"Okay, Mary Sue, where do you want to start?"

She takes a piece of blank paper out of her loose-leaf binder and a pencil out of her purse. Then she slowly writes her name at the top, the date and the page number. Next, she writes the two equations on her paper next to the number one.

"So that's what you know. What do you do now?"

"I have NO idea! You tell me!" Mary Sue says.

Huh? This is so obvious, I think, but I can't tell her that.

Instead I say, "Okay, if x = 4, where else do you see an x?"

"Look, kid, you're supposed to be telling me. You know all the answers. Why are you asking me? With all these stupid letters in a math book, I'm clueless."

She sets down her pencil, and her bright red nail polish shines in the sunlight.

"Hmm, okay, so you don't get variables," I say.

"Hell no."

I take a deep breath and Mary Sue's perfume makes me cough.

"Let me think a minute. Sigh! How can I explain this…"

I get out of my seat and go to the board. I write 3 + x = 5.

"Can you tell me what x is now?"

"X, it's a letter near the end of the alphabet."

She really is clueless, I think.

Instead I say, "Well, yes, but here it stands for a number."

"That's the stupidest thing I ever heard of! Who invented this useless nonsense?"

"I don't know who invented it, but there are times when you need to use letters, because you don't know what the numbers actually are."

"You are not making any sense at all, girl."

I sigh and proceed to explain a few simple equations.

"Mary Sue, you can do this," I try to encourage her.

"That's what you think! Remember I'm dumb at math, especially algebra."

"Maybe I can explain it with a different example. If you think of an equation as a see-saw, and there's a kid and a bag on each side."

I quickly draw a see-saw with stick figures and bags. Under it I write the numbers in the equation she's trying to solve. Finally I see a glimmer of understanding, and I have her write the solution to the first problem on her homework paper. As I'm writing Question #2 with the chalk, I realize that I take so much for granted when I do math.

This is like making a cake from scratch instead of using a cake mix, only much harder. I have to think about every little step.

I point to two equations on the board.

"Okay, Mary Sue, where do we start here?"

"I don't know."

"Sigh! Okay, just like last time, we have two equations. Remember, we substituted the value for one unknown into the second equation."

I coax her along until she comes up with the right answer. Then I make sure she understands that she is subtracting the same thing from both sides of the equation.

"Because, it can get more complicated where you are adding, multiplying or dividing both sides of the equations by the same thing. If you think about keeping the see-saw level, it's a lot easier," I explain.

"Oh yeah, so that's what the teacher means when he says that 'whatever you do to one side, you have to do to the other'."

"Yes!" I exclaim.

Then I glance at the clock. Oh dear, we have fifteen minutes and four problems to go. Mary Sue does the third one all right with just a hint from me. Then, I write the next one on the board, and she gets the procedure right, but drops the minus sign.

"Hah!" A tall dude swaggers into the room with his shoulders back and flips his long black hair with the motion of his head. He pulls open the snaps on his leather jacket showing off his muscular chest under a thin white t-shirt.

Mr. LeCourt stops in mid-sentence during his quiet conversation with Colleen. He looks up and glares at the kid standing in the doorway. After a short pause, Mr.LeCourt says "and you are here in my classroom for what?"

Ignoring Mr. LeCourt, the kid says to Mary Sue "Chickee, here I was worrying for nothin', I thought you had a tutor who was better lookin' than me and smart besides… never woulda guessed it'd be the Pipsqueak! What a joke!"

Chickee? And I thought Vicki, the queen of the smokers, was scary!

"Well, are you ready to go?" he asks Mary Sue, with his leather boots solid on the floor and his hands on his hips.

"We're not done," she tells him. "But I've really had enough!" Mary Sue looks down at her paper, and adds in a quiet voice, "we're only halfway through this homework."

"So you must be Mary Sue's boyfriend," I say quietly, hoping for an introduction.

"Ain't it obvious?" he replies with cutting sarcasm.

"Maybe we can do a little more in home room tomorrow," I say in a quiet tone to Mary Sue.

"C'mon Chickee, my cycle's hot. Let's hit McDonald's. I'm starving." He says in a deep, commanding voice, twisting his wrist as if revving up a motorcycle.

Mary Sue takes her stuff, and follows him obediently.

As I'm gathering up my things, Colleen thanks Mr. LeCourt and says she thinks that the French isn't really so hard. His shiny brown shoes are tapping on the floor.

Then he looks at me and asks, "so how do you feel about tutoring Mary Sue?"

"It's a whole lot harder than I ever expected. We got through half of her homework. But we had to start all over at the beginning. She said she hadn't done anything in math all year. I had no idea that anyone could sit in class day after day and understand absolutely nothing. It's really hard to keep her mind on the math."

"For the first session, it sounds like you did pretty well."

"She has no idea that it's just as hard for me to try to explain what is so obvious! Oops, I better get going or I'll miss the late bus. *Au revoir et merci,* Mr. LeCourt!"

#

I race down the stairs and out the front of the building to the bus. I trip on the bottom step and bump my shin hard.

"Whoa, take it easy there," the bus driver says.

I make it up the three high steps and look around but there are no empty seats. I know that's Sharon's brother sitting by himself in the second row. They always get on the bus together and they look a lot alike. I go over and sit down carefully smoothing my skirt and leaving space between us. I look over as he gives me a slight smile.

"Looks like you made a mess of your leg getting on the bus," he says. "Are you okay?"

"Umm, yes."

"What did you stay after school for?" he asks.

"Umm, I'm tutoring a girl in my homeroom."

"That sounds pretty cool. I'm on the debate team. I like being able to stand up and argue your case like a lawyer. I got a lot of points today, and our team won against Woodson High. "

"Oh, that's great!"

"Yep, it's the challenge that makes it so much fun. Oh, by the way, I'm Tom, Sharon's brother."

"I know." I say, blushing.

You're Anne's sister, right?"

"Yeah. I'm Kenda."

"Oh, time for me to get off here, excuse me."

I stand up and he squeezes past, while I hold my breath. I exhale when he is in the aisle.

He glances back over his shoulder and says "Hello and Bye! See ya 'round."

"Bye…Tom!" I answer, not sure if he heard me.

I sit back down and look out the window as he walks up the driveway to the huge brick house with the four Doric columns, reminding me of Monticello.

The bus careens around the twists and turns of the narrow roads, stopping here and there to let other kids off. Most of the bus is empty now. I move to the seat behind the driver.

"Okay, you can let me off here by the dirt road," I tell him.

It seems strange to be walking up to the house without Annie. The road seems so much longer and the hill steeper than ever, the bruise on my shin makes it even worse. By the time I get home, it's almost five o'clock and I still have lots to study.

Annie comes rushing to the cellar door, firing questions at me before I even get inside.

"How was it? Who are you tutoring? Are you really going to get paid? Oh, yuck, look at your leg! What happened?"

As I'm taking off my coat, I look down at my leg. It's all bruised and has a lump on it the size of a walnut.

"Oh, I slipped getting on the late bus. The usual, huh? But you'll never guess who I'm tutoring. None other than Mary Sue!"

"Mary Sue Parsonfield?"

"Yep! When she walked into the room, her first words were 'You've got to be kidding me!' At first she was acting her usual obnoxious self. But then I guess she realized that she needed help and Mr. LeCourt said just the right thing to her, so she kinda mellowed out, just a bit. I had no idea teaching math could be so hard. Do you believe she hasn't done any homework since the beginning of the year? No wonder she has all 'F's in math! Can you imagine what Dad would say if we even brought home a 'C' in anything but Phys Ed!"

"Sheesh! I thought Mary Sue's parents were pretty good. Why do you think they haven't done anything until now? Do you think there's any hope for her to pass?" Annie asks.

"Well our guidance counselor and her parents must think so if they hired me. But that sure puts a lot on me. Part of the problem is that she's so boy-crazy. Her boyfriend is a biker-dude, complete with the black leather jacket. He's good-looking, but he treats her really badly. I'd rather have no boyfriend than that guy."

We go upstairs to find the stew boiling over on the stove. Annie picks up the pot carefully and moves it to the sink. I turn off the burner, knowing that we'll have to wait until it cools to clean it. At least it's not burnt. I get out the spoons and bowls to set the table. Mom, Dad and Bonnie will be home soon. Annie opens the breadbox and asks if I'd rather have rye or pumpernickel bread with dinner.

Actually, I'd like a slice of plain white Wonder Bread. But Mom and Dad won't buy that. They claim it's not real bread, even though that's what everyone else eats. I opt for pumpernickel; I hate how the rye bread seeds get stuck in your teeth. Annie puts two slices of rye and three of pumpernickel on a plate and starts to get the butter when we hear the sound of tires on the gravel. Just in time.

As Mom walks in, she breathes in and says "Mmm! Dinner sure smells good. You girls are such a great help."

Bonnie is skipping around the living room, leaving a trail of dust in her path.

"Hi Annie. Hi Minnie," Dad says in passing and heads straight to the bathroom.

As soon as we are all seated at dinner, he asks me how my tutoring job went.

"I had no idea it would be so hard! Mary Sue not only hates math, she hates me. But she knows that she has to pass algebra, so she puts up with me. Mary Sue had easy homework and just six problems, but still we only got halfway through. She hasn't done any math homework at all this year, and it's February! Her test is next week. So we have a LOT of work to do!

"Blah! Blah! Blah!" Bonnie grouses.

As soon as I'm finished eating I excuse myself and begin to clear the table and wash the dishes. Most of the time I'm the last one done, but tonight I'm anxious to get to my studying. I am worried about that history test. Thank goodness I was able to borrow notes from Sally, or I'd be dead.

17. SKILLS TEST

The alarm goes off way too early. I have all these medieval characters swirling around in my head. I keep reciting dates and facts to myself as I get dressed and eat. Mom made nice warm oatmeal with cinnamon. Yum, the smell reminds me of apple pie and snickerdoodles.

As Annie and I open the door, the wind almost blows my scarf off. We walk quickly down the road, which runs along the fenced-in pasture of Farmer Johnson. Our wool pleated skirts and woolen knee high socks don't keep our legs very warm. At least we'll be able to turn our backs to the wind when we get to the bus stop. I sure hope the bus comes soon. Jim bounds down the front steps of his house, so we know the bus is just over the hill.

I spend the whole ride worrying about the history test, trying to remember facts about the Crusades, Charlemagne, Roman Empire, and the Battle of Hastings. If all these people are long gone, why do we still care about them? And how do we know all this really happened if the printing press wasn't invented until hundreds of years later?

Soon the bus pulls up to the sidewalk in front of the high school and I glance out the window. *Yikes!* Vicki and the whole smoking gang, along with Parsonfield's boyfriend and a few other tough-looking guys are milling around near the bus. Are they waiting for me? I duck down while the other kids pile off the bus until it's almost empty. The driver stands up, stretches his arms over his head and yawns as I peek above the seat. Then he looks straight at me.

"What'sa matter, kid? You look like you just saw a ghost. You all right?"

"Umm, yes, I guess," I say as I slowly stand up.

"Time to get off, I've got junior high kids to pick up."

As he looks out the door, he sees the whole gang, and then he looks back at me. The bus driver's heavy leather boots stomp down the steps and he tells them all to stop hanging around his bus and get into the building. I keep far enough back so they don't see me.

"Guess she's not comin' to school today," I hear Mary Sue's boyfriend say. The gang moves like a bunch of chickens heading to the feeder, not very orderly but the whole mass is going in the same direction, away from me.

"Phew! Thanks," I whisper to the bus driver and slowly inch down the steps into the side door of the school by the library. Luckily, it's unlocked and I pull hard against the wind to get it open. I rush upstairs to my locker and then to homeroom. I open my history notes and begin some last-minute cramming. My concentration is broken by the loud surprised voice of Mary Sue.

"What are you doing here? How the hell did you *get* here?"

Mr. LeCourt clears his throat, and says "*Pardonnez-moi?*"

"Oh yeah," Mary Sue says, "how the heck did you get here?"

"I walked." I reply quietly, knowing exactly what she means.

"That's not what I'm talking about, "Mary Sue retorts.

"What? Is something wrong?"

"Never mind," she snaps.

"Did you look at any of your algebra last night?" I ask.

"Bet you think I'm gonna say No. But surprise! I did problem 4 all by myself, wanna see?"

I force myself to say "yes."

Mary Sue flips open her binder and shows me the page of algebra problems. I can't help but smile. She got it right! And she even started the first word problem.

"Hey, not bad. You even got the first of two equations right for the word problem," I say.

"So now what do I do?" Mary Sue asks impatiently.

I read the problem and give her a few hints.

We're being watched. I try to glance up without really moving my head too much. Then my eyes meet Mr. LeCourt's round smiling face. I sigh with relief. Mary Sue writes something, then erases, writes something else, then some more. Finally she shows me her paper.

"Okay, you've almost got it. Think about the see-saw. Subtract the same thing from both sides of the equation."

"The answer's 16, right?" Mary Sue asks.

The bell rings before I can reply. I gather up my stuff, but Mary Sue stands squarely in front of me waiting for me to tell her it's correct. When I do, we both head for the gym.

I'm shivering as I stand in the locker room. Girls snap up ugly blue gym suits, lockers slam, shouts fly across the room and echo back. As soon as I'm dressed I rush into the gym where it's warmer and quieter. Miss Ditch appears out of nowhere.

"Panic! What's the rush? Surely, you're not anxious to start exercises and your skills test, now are you?"

I come to a screeching halt in front of her.

"Skills test? NO! not today?!"

"Yes, the deck tennis unit is over...after today."

Soon the whole class is in the gym and lined up for coordination exercises. I completely forgot about this skills test, my mind was so absorbed with history coming up.

"All right pair up!" Miss Ditch brings my mind back to gym with her booming voice. I look for a friend, but Parsonfield comes over to me with a grin on her face.

"I'll be your partner, Panic."

"What? Why me?"

"Hah! It's my turn to show *you* how to do something." Parsonfield sneers.

Boy, am I dead!

"All right girls. Here's how this works. One of you takes the ring first and does 5 serves. The other with the clipboard writes the scores depending on where the serve lands: diagonal, in bounds 10 points; out of bounds or in the net 0; and straight court in bounds, 5. Then trade places. Next do 5 returns, 10 points each if it's over the net, otherwise it's a 0. Record them and turn in your sheets."

As soon as Miss Ditch finishes the instructions, Parsonfield grabs the clipboard and tosses me the ring.

My scores are: first serve–10, second–10, next–10, next–5, and the last one–another 10. I nod, yes, this is good. Mary Sue picks up the ring and thrusts her hand out with the clipboard. I reach for it and just as I almost have it in my hand, she pulls it away and lets it fall on the floor with a clatter. Girls jump, look my way, and giggle.

"Panic! Are you causing that commotion over there?" Miss Ditch asks.

"No, I mean, not really. It's no commotion. I just dropped the clipboard."

"All right then. Let's get on with the skills tests." Miss Ditch shouts.

Mary Sue grins and proceeds to do 5 perfect serves.

"That's a 50! Hah! Beat you! And who says I can't do math?" Mary Sue's sarcasm stings.

She then tells me to serve her the ring for her returns. I send it across the net in a nice arc. Her hand is right there for the catch and she instantly flings it back for 10 points. Next serve I send it over to the other side of the court, and just as easily she throws it back for another 10 points. The next three returns are equally well executed. I'm impressed, a perfect score.

"Cool! That was impressive," I say.

"No big deal! Now it's your turn." As she makes figure eights with her right arm outstretched and the ring firmly grasped in her hand, she grins.

"Ready?" the ring comes flying at me so fast it's a blur.

"Zero!" she shouts loud enough for everyone to hear.

I try to ignore her as I pick up the blue ring and slowly pass it over the net to her.

She snatches it out of the air and sends it right back at me in a flash. It hits the floor before I can get anywhere near the blue thing. Now I know why she wanted to be my partner. There are three more throws that all turn to zeros.

"Hah! Panic got a 45!" She announces to the whole gym and everyone in it.

I hear the 45 echo over and over in my ears. My whole brain shuts down. I am so furious! But I don't dare tell Miss Ditch that this is totally unfair. If I had another partner, I could definitely do better.

I scream at Mary Sue, "How can you be so mean? You know *no one* could return those rings you threw at me! Why can't you be nice to me, just once? After all, I am helping you in math!"

She pretends she doesn't hear me amidst the noise of everyone racing to the locker room. I follow the crowd putting one foot in front of the other, looking down at the floor. In the locker room I claim my towel, shower, and get dressed. I speak to no one. There is nothing more to say.

Thank heavens for geometry class. The Captain greets me with a whispered "You okay, Kenda?"

"Umm, yes, I guess," I mutter.

"That doesn't sound very convincing."

"Just another awful gym test and a big history test next period."

"You'll do fine," he says with an encouraging smile as I take my seat.

Before I know it, the bell rings. *Yikes, I'm not ready for history.* I gather up my stuff and make my way through the hall of pushing, shoving bodies to Mr. Jackson's room. I hurry to my seat and pull out my notes to cram just a little more junk in my brain before the test. I reach in my purse and pull out my lucky pen. The teacher picks up a stack of papers with purple ink on them, and passes out the mimeographed tests.

I finish the short answer questions easily. Now for the essay *"The Crusades was a Holy War. Compare and contrast this to a war in our century."* Boy, am I glad I didn't read this first. What are you supposed to write for that?

I can't say anything about the Vietnam War because we really don't know *why* we are fighting it. I write something about World War II, and add that all these wars are wrong. People should just believe in the constitution and the rights of others and then they would have no reason to fight.

I really like this teacher and his class, but I *hate* his tests. They're impossible! There really are no answers to these essay questions.

18. ANOTHER TUTORING SESSION

Soon classes are over and I go to Mr.LeCourt's's room to face Mary Sue for another tutoring session. How could I get myself into this? She's so pushy and bossy with me and I'm supposed to be teaching *her*. When we lived next door to each other she was five, only a month younger than Annie, yet she acted like she was in charge all the time, even when she was at our house. But it's strange how totally different Mary Sue acts around her boyfriend. I look at the clock. It's 3:05. She's late. I begin tapping the eraser end of my pencil on the desk; somehow moving even a small part of my body makes me feel a little less nervous. *Why should I be nervous?*

"What do think you're doing? Practicing coordination exercises with your fingers? Hah! a 45 on your skills test! Why don't you just give up in there?" Mary Sue asks as she saunters in the door, and plops herself in the chair next to mine.

She reeks of cigarette smoke. That's enough for me to know why she's late. I don't want to start off with a confrontation, so I try to ignore the smell and the tardiness.

"So, I suppose you want to know why I'm late. Well I stopped for a smoke, figured I'd need it to survive another hour with you and math."

"Okay, let's get started on your algebra," I say.

"Don't you know it's Friday? We should be partying not studying."

Mustering my most commanding voice, I say, "look Mary Sue, you know we need all the time we can get to prepare you for next week's test if you're going to pass Algebra."

"All right," Mary Sue groans. "Where do we start?"

"Let's take a look at the homework we worked on yesterday and be sure you understand it," I say.

"We went over it in class."

"Yes, but are you sure you understand it?"

"The teacher was real surprised that I did at least some of it, so he had me put the second problem on the board. The old Colonel and the class made a big deal about it."

"Good, but what about the word problems?"

"I get how they did them, but I still don't have a clue where to begin by myself. But what do you care?"

"Because it's my job to help you."

"So, that doesn't mean you give a damn."

"C'mon, Mary Sue. If I didn't want you to pass math, I wouldn't be here. Now stop asking questions and let's get to work. Do you have homework for Monday?"

"Yeah, he gave us a whole huge problem set. It's supposed to help us review for the test."

"Okay, take it out and we'll start on it. Whatever we don't get done, you have to promise me you'll at least try all the problems over the weekend. That way we'll have a chance of finishing them before the test."

Slowly, she opens her binder and takes out some purple mimeographed papers that are stapled together, and tosses them on the desk.

"We'll never get through all this," she says. "It's impossible! Who are we kidding? Let's just quit and go home. It *is* Friday."

"Mary Sue, you can't give up. You can do this. But you gotta try!" I say trying to hide my impatience with her.

"Why don't you just write the first problem on the board?"

Snatching the papers she goes to the board and writes a simple equation with one unknown value.

"Okay," I begin. "What are you going to do next?"

"Get rid of the two. Subtract it here."

"And…?"

"Oh yeah and on the other side of the equation."

"That's the idea. Keep going."

She writes two more lines on the board and comes up with 15.

"Is that right?"

"Yep! There you go. Now move on to number two."

She solves that one without a hint. Whew!

Number three is the same, but her subtraction is wrong.

"You've got the right idea, but how much is 19 from 31? If you add 2 to 19, do you get 31?"

"See I told you I couldn't do math. This is stupid." Mary Sue throws the chalk on the floor.

"It's just a little thing." I say, feeling her slipping away. "Subtract 19 from 31 again," I tell her.

"Just give me the answer!" She shouts at me.

"You can do this." I say trying hard not to shout back at her. I pick up a piece of broken chalk and write 31, under it I put -19, draw a line, and hand her the chalk.

She tries again and gets the correct answer. "Are you satisfied now?"

"Good, see you can do it. Let's go on to number four," I say.

"This is a word problem. Forget it!"

"Nope. You can figure this out. If you practice these they'll get easier and you'll be able to do them, just like you did number two," I say trying to be convincing.

"Oh, all right." She reads the problem, and says, "I know John's age now is 35 and in 5 years John will be twice as old as Sally. I really could care less how old Sally will be then. I don't even know her!"

"Let's pretend Sally is Vicki, then."

She scribbles some numbers on the board and blurts out "20, am I right?"

"I'll tell you once you show me the equations," I reply.

"Okay! Okay!"

She sounds exasperated, but gets them correct.

"Yess! You solved it!" I'm more excited than she is.

Just as I start to think that Mary Sue is feeling good about her work, she jumps up and shouts "Rod! My Hot Rod! You saved me!"

I look up to see Mary Sue's boyfriend in his tight jeans and black leather jacket in the doorway. He brushes his hand through his straight, jet-black hair, and stands tall with his shoulders back.

He says, "No problem, Chickee. I still can't believe you're doin' this—and on a Friday!"

Mary Sue turns to me. "Oh yeah, my Dad says I gotta give you this." She tosses a small white envelope on the desk.

"Tell him 'thank you,' and please at least try and do as many problems as you can this weekend. Give yourself just an hour each day. Otherwise we won't have enough time to prepare for that test next week."

"That sure is asking a lot from my Chickee." Rod glares at me, and they turn and leave with his arm around her.

#

I race to my locker and out to the late bus. It's almost empty today, and there's no Tom. I was really hoping he'd be here. I guess there's no debate team on Friday. I reach in my purse and take out the envelope with Kenda written on the front. Opening it slowly and carefully, I find three worn one-dollar bills and a little scrap of paper. It reads, "Thank you Kenda. Mr. P." I fold it up, stick the note and money in the envelope, and put it back in my purse. My pay is three dollars for almost three hours of exhausting verbal tug-of-wars with Mary Sue. But I feel proud, I've earned every penny of it.

"Hey Miss, don't you get off around here?"

It's the bus driver's voice that shakes me from my thoughts. I look up.

"Oh, yeah. Actually, back there."

As the driver stops at Farmer Johnson's driveway, "Sorry," he says, "but you've only been on this bus once or twice before, and I figured you'd speak up."

"It's okay," I mumble, "have a good weekend."

After getting off the bus, I make my way to the fence covered in honey suckle vines and squeeze between the posts to our road. As I trudge home, I think how much longer this walk is when Annie's not with me. She's waiting for me at the cellar door when I finally get there.

"So, how was your day? Did Mary Sue treat you any better? She oughta be so thankful to you that you are willing to help her."

"Not really, 'cause she knows I'm getting paid and she thinks it's easy for me. The math is, but she's so hard to tutor. All she thinks about is boys and smoking! She showed up late and her boyfriend, Rod came early, so I really didn't tutor her for the full hour. But she paid me."

I set all my stuff down by the door and reach in my purse for the envelope. I pull out the money and give Annie a dollar.

"I'll get you the other fifty cents when we get upstairs." I show her the note from Mary Sue's father.

"Nice that he appreciates what you are doing," Annie says.

Soon it's dinnertime and we are at the table.

Dad asks, "Minnie, how was work today?"

"It's harder than I ever imagined." I tell him how difficult Mary Sue is.

"It'll get easier, you'll see, Minnie."

"What are you talking about? Kennie, you go to school, not work." Bonnie is puzzled.

"It's not school, Bonnie. I am tutoring a girl after school. That's what I get paid for."

"What's tutoring?"

"When you are like the teacher, but with only one student."

"Why only one kid, where are all the others?"

"They've gone home already, 'cause it's after regular school."

"Why would anyone want to spend more time at school, especially to have *you* for a teacher?"

"First of all Mary Sue had no choice for a teacher. You never do. Second, she is failing math and needs help if she's going to pass."

"She must be really stupid!"

"No, she just hasn't been doing her work or trying, so she's way behind."

"Well, that sounds stupid to me."

Bonnie always has to have the last word, and Mom yells at me whenever I stand up to her, so I just let it go.

Mom talks about how she is happy that it's Friday. They have so much going on at work that she had only ten minutes for lunch. Her boss is good and treats her well. I am so glad the conversation is about something other than tutoring Mary Sue.

I finish my corn and think about how we planted the seeds, weeded, watered, picked, shucked and froze this corn last summer. It still tastes really good and is so much more fun to eat on the cob than with a fork. When everyone is done eating, Annie and I start to clear the table, so we can get the dishes washed and put away.

"Bonnie, you could at least help clear the table," I suggest.

"Suppose I don't wanna?" she replies standing next to her chair with her hands on her hips and her lips pressed firmly together.

"Maybe Annie and I don't feel like doing the dishes either, but we help. Otherwise Mom would have to do it, and she works hard all week."

Bonnie looks at Mom. She nods her head and Bonnie slowly picks up her plate and silverware and takes it to the kitchen.

19. MONDAY

It's another typical Monday in homeroom. The usual smiling face of Mr. LeCourt greets us. I look around, but don't see Mary Sue.

When she arrives after the bell, I notice that her make-up is a lot heavier than usual and the right side of her face looks a little puffy and a darker color, almost like she's hiding a bruise. I'm afraid to say anything.

"Whatcha staring at Pipsqueak?" she asks in a nasty tone.

"Nothing. I'm just glad you're here."

"Yeah, so you can torture me some more after school."

Mr. LeCourt furrows his brow and turns his head away from us, but I can tell he's still listening to our conversation.

I can't take my eyes off Mary Sue's face.

"You should know it's not polite to stare," she says, pointing her finger at me.

"Okay," I reply.

Mr. LeCourt comes to the rescue. "Mary Sue, we just wanted to be sure you'll be coming for that extra help since your algebra test is this week."

"Yeah, thanks. I'll be here at three o'clock."

True to her word, Mary Sue arrives on time after school.

"Okay Panic," she says as she drops her binder on the desk. "I'm desperate. How about you take this test for me?"

"Mary Sue, I'll help you, but you know, I can't take it for you. Now let's see what you did over the weekend."

Mary Sue keeps her head down, and I almost think there's a tear in the corner of her eye; it must be my imagination. Slowly she takes the packet of purple papers from her binder. There are a lot of erasures and scribbles on them. "I tried," she says. "I really did."

We quietly read over the problems together. She gets the equations right, but her division is wrong.

"Mary Sue, you got this one almost right. You seem to be getting the hang of doing the same thing to both sides of the equation. But when you divide this side by 12, what do you get?"

"Oh, I don't know. You tell me. I can't get the right answer."

"Sure you can, just start your 12 times table 12,…?"

"*Okay,*" her impatient voice continues with "24, 36…, 48…60."

"So that was the 5th number in the sequence, so 60 divided by 12 is?"

"Yeah, five."

"Yes, that's the answer. Y'know it would really help you a lot if you made up flash cards for your math facts. I know it sounds 'little-kid-ish', but once you get them down really fast, you'll get a lot more answers right and quickly."

"C'mon, you know we don't have time for that. This test is in four days."

"All right, on to number seven." I read it quickly and look at her solution.

"Yes, Mary Sue. This one is right!"

We continue and I am amazed that she's so cooperative. We finish going through all the problems. I look at her bruised face with the worn off make-up.

"You must be pretty smart to learn all this in less than a week," I say smiling. "I still think the flash cards would help a lot too."

Mr. LeCourt, who had been grading papers quietly at his desk, pops his cheery face up. "Would you two like some index cards? I have plenty."

"Yes, they'd be perfect." For once I reply before Mary Sue can say no.

I get up to take the cards, and begin writing on the front of them. Starting with the three times table, I skip the easy ones like 3 x 1 and 3 x 2. Then I hand her each card to put the answer on the back. She actually seems to like this because she knows most of the answers. It only takes a few minutes to get through 12 x 12. Then I take her stack and check the answers she put on the back.

"Great! Mary Sue. We finished those in no time! Now you need to drill yourself on the ones I corrected," I say.

Mary Sue covers her bruise and says, "Yeah, sure thanks." Then she smiles.

As we gather up her packet and the cards, Rod comes swaggering in.

"So here you are again with smart-ass pipsqueak! Didn't you learn your lesson yesterday?" he snarls at her.

Mr. LeCourt's perennial smile is gone. He stands up, with his feet firmly on the floor and his shoulders back. He looks directly at Rod.

"Excuse me," he says to Rod. "This is my classroom. There will be none of that language in here. Furthermore, you are not to treat my students like that."

"Yeah! What're you gonna do about it? In case you hadn't noticed, I'm bigger than all of you!" Rod laughs as he moves closer to Mr. LeCourt.

Mr. LeCourt quietly steps to the intercom and pushes the button in three short taps, three long ones and three more short ones. Then a voice comes on " Mr. LeCourt, check."

"What the hell are you doing?" Rod growls at the teacher.

"Just testing my intercom," Mr. LeCourt says.

"I'm talking to my girl here and what I say and how I say it is none of your damn business."

"In my classroom, it is," Mr. LeCourt says firmly.

Rod wastes no time. He grabs Mary Sue by the hair and yanks her out into the hallway.

"You give me grief again," he shouts at her, "and I'll slap you silly and you know I ain't kiddin'!"

I gasp, holding my breath in fear for Mary Sue. Then I look at Mr. LeCourt. He is perfectly calm and composed as he walks to the doorway.

Suddenly, there's a scuffle in the hall. The assistant principal and a tall, hulking guidance counselor have Rod between them, with his arms crossed behind his back. He is shouting obscenities at Mary Sue. She looks toward us, then back at him. Other teachers poke their heads out of their doorways. Mary Sue turns her back on us and slowly walks down the hall after Rod.

I finally take a deep breath and look at Mr. LeCourt. We both sigh with relief.

"Well, I guess we've had enough excitement for one day. You better run and catch your bus!"

I look at the clock, it's a minute after four. I run to my locker and grab my coat. I go as fast as I can down the stairs and get there just as the driver closes the door. He opens it again. Whew, just made it!

All the way home I think about Mary Sue. Would Rod really hurt her if she didn't do what he wanted? Could he have "slapped her in the face" over the weekend? What if Mr. LeCourt was out of the room when he came in? What happened in the office? I can only wonder. Something tells me that Mary Sue's algebra test isn't her only worry. I can't wait to tell Annie about it when I get home.

#

I run down the long straight part of the road and up the hill. When I get to the cellar door, Annie isn't there, but the door is unlocked. I rush inside and drop my stuff.

"Annie! Annie! You'll never guess what happened this afternoon."

She's not in the rec room, so I go quickly up the stairs hanging on to the bannister.

"Annie! Annie! Are you here?"

"Shhh!"

I find her talking on the phone.

"Yes, but my sister's home. I'll see you in school tomorrow. Bye for now."

"Who was that?"

"Just a friend from school."

"A boy?"

"Actually, yes. But don't breathe a word to Bonnie or Mom or Dad. I really don't want to deal with a million questions: *Where does he live? What does his father do for work? How many siblings does he have? What's his religion?* Blah, blah, blah."

That night I have a terrible dream. I see Rod standing in homeroom threatening us, and the intercom is ripped off the wall. Mr. LeCourt is crouched under his desk. I try to run for the door to get help, but Rod grabs my arm and twists it until it feels like it's going to break. I try to scream, but nothing comes out. He starts shaking me.

No, wait, it's Annie shaking me.

"What's the matter? You are screaming in your sleep! That must be some nightmare! Are you okay?"

"Yes. Thank goodness I was dreaming. Rod was coming at us and there was no one to protect us. Do you really think he hurt Mary Sue?" I ask.

"I don't know, but we both better get some sleep."

20. A BAD SITUATION

When the alarm goes off on Tuesday I have to drag myself out of bed. Imagining the dark circles under my eyes even before I look in the mirror, I have a strange feeling that this is not going to be an ordinary day.

A few hours later, I get to homeroom where Mr. LeCourt is anything but cheery. His forehead is wrinkled and he looks like a tired, worried old man.

"*Bonjour*," I say to him.

He barely answers. Something *is* wrong.

I look around for Mary Sue. She's not in the room. Even after the bell rings at the end of homeroom, she still doesn't show up.

"Mr. LeCourt, where's Mary Sue?" I ask.

"I don't know," he replies quietly.

All day Mary Sue is in the back of my mind. As much as I hate her attitude and I hate the way she treats me, I am worried about her.

When the school day ends, there's still no sign of Mary Sue.

The next day, she shows up in homeroom. She brushes a stray hair off her forehead and I notice her black eye, caked over with make-up that still doesn't cover it.

I go over to her and whisper, "Oh, Mary Sue, what happened?"

"Shut up!" she says tightly, "Don't say a word to anyone, Pipsqueak! This mess is your fault."

"But what happened?"

"Don't you understand what 'Shut up' means?" she whispers harshly in my face.

I scoot my chair back away from her, and look up at Mr. LeCourt, busy explaining to some kid why he failed a French test.

Leaning toward me, Mary Sue says in her deep smoker's voice, "It's none of your business! Got that? Now leave me alone!"

"Okay," I manage to whisper.

For the rest of homeroom, we both sit silently. I wonder, am I supposed to meet her this afternoon to tutor her again? Or are we through? As the bell rings, I dread going to the gym. She has a way of projecting her anger at me there. I avoid her in the hall and go directly to my gym locker.

"Parsonfield" Miss Ditch's voice booms above the chatter. "Meet me in my office."

I wonder if she's in trouble with Miss Ditch too.

"Nick, get everyone in the gym and start on exercises!" Miss Ditch shouts as she pokes her head back in the locker room.

We all meander into the gym and line up. Nick does as she was asked. We do exercises for ten minutes, then fifteen. There's still no sign of Miss Ditch or Mary Sue.

"I think we've done enough exercises," Nick says. "Let's get the basketballs and do some drills." She leads off and we are enjoying the slower pace.

"What happened to Parsonfield?" someone asks.

"I heard there's a restraining order against her boyfriend. Her Dad was furious and called the police."

"Yeah, I think he beat her up."

"I heard it had something to do with her trying to be better than him in math."

I hold my breath and almost want to see Miss Ditch come in to stop these rumors. I can't help but feel at least partly responsible, even though I have no idea what a restraining order is.

Finally Miss Ditch comes in, looking a bit frazzled. "All right, Girls! That's it for today. Hit the showers!"

What is going on? No sign of Mary Sue. We all go to the showers. When I come out the grade book is lying open on the bench by the door with checks by all of our names for today. Whatever it is, Miss Ditch is being nice to all of us.

I don't see Mary Sue for the rest of the day. After school I stop in Mr. LeCourt's room and ask him if I should stay to tutor Mary Sue or go home on my regular bus.

"I wouldn't wait for her, at least not today. Please don't say anything about her. The situation is bad and could get worse if we're not careful."

"Okay, Mr. LeCourt, you have my word."

On the bus there is the usual chatter and a few kids are talking about Mary Sue. I know there is something serious going on and I'm beginning to think that Rod is a *really* bad guy.

On the walk home, Annie keeps asking if I know anything about Mary Sue. I really want to talk about her, but I remember my promise to Mr. LeCourt.

It's a whole week before Mary Sue is in homeroom again. She walks in slowly, with her hair hanging down straight. Her nails aren't polished and she doesn't have any lipstick on. Mr. LeCourt welcomes her with a cheery 'Hello! We missed you, but I'm happy to hear the good news about your algebra test."

I look up at Mary Sue, surprised. "What? Did you pass?" I ask her.

"Yeah! I just remembered the see-saw and got a D+. The teacher said a few more sessions on those word problems and I would have done just fine. I worked hard at all those review sheets, so don't start getting it in your head to take credit for it, Pipsqueak."

"That's great!" I tell her. Do you want any more tutoring sessions?"

"No, *I* don't. But my Dad says we gotta keep this up. So I guess I'll see you this afternoon."

Later that day, we meet in Mr. LeCourt's room. As the math seems to get easier, Mary Sue shows less attitude. I'm glad, it's a lot better for me too. We work until a few minutes before four o'clock and Rod doesn't show up to give her a ride. After I get on the bus, I see Mary Sue walking home alone. I'm glad for that, but disappointed that the debate team didn't meet today. I was really hoping to see Tom again.

21. SOFTBALL

Mr. LeCourt's disposition seems to have rubbed off on the world. It's sunny and almost everyone is in a good mood. As I go into homeroom, I hear whispers in the hall.

"I'm sure. My Dad's a cop and *he'd* know if Rod was in jail. Mary Sue's no gem, but she doesn't deserve that jerk," one of our football players says, holding his hand partly over his mouth.

"Yeah, but she's still upset about it all. Her Dad called the police. You'd think with Mary Sue's Dad bein' a preacher, he'd be able to talk some sense into the two of them," a cheerleader replies.

Mary Sue comes into the room, her head down, and pancake make-up is thick on her face. I notice that it goes all the way down her neck. She shuffles her feet as she walks and doesn't even look my way when she sits down next to me.

Mr. LeCourt comes over to her and whispers, "Is everything all right, Mary Sue?"

No reply, just a nod and a blink, then a tear starts to roll down her cheek. Mary Sue brushes it away quickly.

"If you want to talk, I'm free second period, so just come on in." Mr. LeCourt says in a soft, kind voice.

I want to ask Mary Sue to tell me everything, but I don't think she wants to talk, and certainly not to me!

School is a comfortable routine now, but I still hate gym class. It looks like we might be going outside today, so that should be better. I get to the locker room and take out my gym suit that Annie was nice enough to iron for me yesterday so I could finish my term paper for English. As I take it out of the brown paper bag, it's so stiff, it could stand up all by itself. When I put it on, it even crinkles. What was Annie thinking? She must have drowned it in starch. It's hard to pretend that nothing is wrong. I hold my torso upright moving only my arms and legs, feeling like a robot walking into the gym. Girls start giggling. Oh no!

We line up for exercises...I still can't do those coordination exercises. I know all the positions, but can't keep up with the count. So I head for the back and try to get as far away from everyone as I can.

Miss Ditch looks at me with a raised eyebrow. "Something wrong, Panic?"

"Umm, no Miss Ditch."

"You sure?"

"Yes."

"Well okay then. Let's get moving!" her voice echoes through the gym.

"One, Two, Three,..."

With every move I make, all the girls around me start giggling.

Miss Ditch shouts "Nick get up here and lead these exercises."

As Nick goes to the front, Miss Ditch stomps quickly toward me. I freeze.

"Now what's going on back here?"

I close my mouth and don't move a muscle, barely breathing.

"Someone tell me what's so funny!" she demands.

After a long pause, Lyman says, "It's her gym suit."

"Yeah, what about it? Looks fine to me," Miss Ditch says loudly.

"Just listen," Lyman says.

Miss Ditch tilts her head in my direction, but doesn't hear a thing. I am hoping she'll just go away thinking it was some cricket in my corner of the gym. She stands firmly with her little brown eyes piercing through me. I look away, pretending that there's something on the floor. But she keeps her gaze fixed on me. The exercises continue in the front of the gym, but the cluster of girls around me just stand there hiding their smiles. Finally Miss Ditch steps away and heads toward the front of the gym. I sigh with relief and take a deep breath.

"All right! Y'all in the back, resume these exercises." When I take the next position, the crinkling starts, and so do the giggles. As I finally get to the count of eight, I'm two steps behind everyone and the gym is silent except for the klop of my shoes on the floor and the crinkle of my over-starched gym suit.

"Panic! Now, I've not only seen everything, but I've heard it."

Laughter echoes through the gym.

Miss Ditch tells us, "Today, we'll head out to the field and start our softball unit. I know you didn't play softball in Junior High School, because equipment for girls' gym classes isn't a priority. But, most of you played softball at your neighborhood parks, and some of you did baseball in gym. So, I'm handing out a sheet of rules. Let's move on out!"

"Panic! Go get the rest of the equipment. You can at least make yourself useful," Miss Ditch says. She picks up a bag of baseball gloves and heaves it over her shoulder.

I go to the equipment room next to the locker room and look around. Let's see, bats, bases and balls. I pick up one of the balls the size of a grapefruit, it's hard as a rock. This can't be a *softball.* So I continue to look around. I sense that time is going by, but I can't find any soft balls. What should I do? Take these out there and have everyone laugh? Just bring the bats and say I can't carry anything more? As I'm debating with myself, Mason comes in. "Ditch wants to know what's takin' you so long."

"I can't carry everything without dropping something. Can you get the balls?" I grab the bats and bases and smile to myself.

Mason picks up the hard 'grapefruits' and says, "we'd better run! Ditch is really in a bad mood by now. She wasn't happy when I left."

When we get out to the field, Miss Ditch is shouting louder than I've ever heard her. "Panic! What took you so long? Were you waiting for the class to be over?"

All the other girls are glaring at me.

"What happened?" I ask.

Lyman gasps between her words “We’ve been out here running laps… while you were fooling around in there. Thanks a lot!”

“I’m sorry… really I am.”

“All right girls, time for drills. Take a glove. Get in two lines and start throwing and catching these softballs.”

Girls drag themselves to the sack of gloves that Miss Ditch brought to the field and then they get into lines about ten paces apart. The balls are handed down one row. Nick throws hers to Renee who’s directly across from her. All the other girls start throwing theirs back and forth. I feel so clumsy with this big mitt on my right hand. As I look down at the huge leather monster of a glove, I wonder if it’s too big, or if it’s supposed to be like this. Suddenly a ball hits me in the arm. “OUCH!” I shriek. *Nothing soft about that ball!*

“Panic! You are supposed to CATCH the ball, not just stand there and let it hit you. …Well… pick it up and throw it back!” Miss Ditch yells as everyone looks over and laughs.

I try to pick it up with my right hand, but the huge leather excuse for a hand can’t. So I reach down with my left hand, and then put it into the center of the glove. *Now how am I supposed to throw this thing?* Still holding the ball with my left hand I raise the mitt and ball, lean forward, and move my wounded right arm forward at the elbow. The ball goes all of about four feet in front of me.

Laughter and giggles surround me now.

I think of the poem ‘Ladybug, Ladybug, fly away home.’ I wish I could turn into a ladybug and fly far away from here.

Miss Ditch comes over to me. “Panic! Are you right or left-handed?”

“Right,” I squeak, a bit confused, wondering why she’s asking me that now.

“Panic, the glove should be on your left hand, so you can throw with the right. You picked up the only lefty mitt in the bag.” Miss Ditch sighs and shakes her head.

“Don’t just stand there lookin’. Go and get a proper glove, then get back here and throw that ball to your partner.”

Miss Ditch looks up at the sky. “What did I do to deserve this one?” she asks to no one in particular.

Then she looks at her watch. “We are really late today, thanks to our bat-girl, Panic. Would someone remind me to fire her next time?”

As I head for the bag of gloves, I almost turn around and tell her there’s no need to fire me. I’d be happy to quit.

22. A BRIGHTER NOTE

I hurry to my geometry class. It's great to see the Captain and be on the other side of the school, away from Miss Ditch.

"So how's my favorite tutor doing today?" the Captain asks.

"Oh fine, I guess, except I'm such a klutz in gym class."

"Well, on a brighter note, I hear that Mary Sue is passing algebra, so you must be doing something right. We all know she's not very motivated in math. If you keep up the good work she'll make it through algebra. It's also a great boost to her confidence."

"Thanks," I tell him. The Captain has no idea how much I need his words of encouragement. But suddenly I remember that Mary Sue wasn't in gym class. I wonder if she'll be here after school.

The morning passes quickly and when I get to the cafeteria, I see Mary Sue surrounded by Vicki and her gang. I don't dare go anywhere near them, but I am a bit relieved to see Mary Sue.

I get my lunch and sit down by Sally, Margy, Cathy and Sharon. It isn't long before Erik comes over. Some kids still get up and move, but we're okay with him at our table. I think it's a lot worse to be rude and mean than to sit by someone who isn't too smart or good looking. He never bothers anyone. Erik just sits and eats, picks up his tray and shuffles over to the conveyor belt with his dirty dishes when he's done.

Sharon says she's staying after school for her FNA meeting.

"What's that?" Erik asks.

"Future Nurses of America, you know, like FTA is Future Teachers. Kenda, are you in Future Teachers?"

"No way! I've had enough of teaching trying to tutor Mary Sue."

"So what club are you in?"

"None. About all I'd be good for is FOMA."

"Huh? What's that?"

"Future Old Maids of America."

"Is that really a club?" Erik asks.

"Of course not," Sharon says and everyone laughs.

"It's true. I'm definitely headed for Old Maidhood. The boys all ignore me, except maybe Tom and Mike. But they're nice to everyone and surely they'll marry sweet, good-looking girls who have a lot of personality too. I am so uncomfortable around boys; they're like alien creatures to me."

#

After a few more classes, I find myself back in Mr. LeCourt's classroom, where my school day began.

"Hi Kenda! Is Mary Sue coming this afternoon?"

"Gee, Mr. LeCourt, I was hoping you knew. I thought I'd just come here in case she does. If she doesn't I'll just do my own homework until it's time to catch the late bus. Is that okay with you?"

"*Mai oui!*"

I take out my English book and start memorizing the beginning of *The Canterbury Tales*. What strange language: "*Whan that April with its shoorest sote…*" But it's kinda fun when you start to get the hang of it.

The Leprechaun sits at his desk grading papers. The corners of his mouth turn up effortlessly, as he looks up.

"Do you mind if I play a some music?"

"No, not at all," I reply.

He pushes his chair back and goes to the tape player, with a reel in his hand. In a few minutes, a beautiful soft tune comes pouring out, and as I listen I realize the words are all in French.

I go back to *The Canterbury Tales*. With the music playing, it's wonderfully calm and relaxing here.

Suddenly Mary Sue bursts into the room. "Yeah, I'm here," she announces. Her hair's a mess, the hem of her skirt is torn and one of her socks droops down on her scuffed saddle shoe.

"Good grief! You look like you've come through a hurricane!" I blurt out.

"I expected a nicer greeting from you." Mary Sue replies.

"We *are* glad to see you," Mr. LeCourt says.

"You don't *really* care. But I am here. You know I got a C on my last math test and Dad says I gotta keep doin' this. Maybe I shoulda' just kept on flunking, and then I wouldn't have to do this boring stuff after a whole day of classes. And Kenda, your life is a joke, you know."

"Huh? What do you mean?"

"You just don't understand anything about the real world, I saw you with that ugly boy and those nerdy girls at lunch. You'll never have a normal life, girl!"

I grit my teeth and say, "my friends are nice, which is more than I can say for yours. And there's nothing wrong with being smart. I can do math and help you with algebra, so let's get on with it."

She drops her algebra book on the desk and glares at me.

"Well, what's for homework?" I ask her.

Shuffling through papers stuffed in her binder, she pulls out a piece of lined paper. As she slides her bottom in the chair, her long thin fingers with bright red nail polish wrap around a pencil.

"Okay, let's see what page 189 is all about. Why don't you read question four?"

"Okay, read question four." She mimics me in a babyish voice.

"Are we going to work on this math or not?" I ask.

"Just quit bossing me around," she retorts, looking me in the eye.

Her attention goes to the problem in the book for just a minute. Then she looks up at Mr. LeCourt. "I'm trying to concentrate here. You can turn off that foreign music," she demands.

"Don't you think you could ask me a little nicer? It is my classroom, you know."

"All right! Please turn it off."

Mr. LeCourt pushes the button and the music stops.

Our session continues and Mary Sue is doing most of the problems herself, stopping every now and then to ask me a question. I'm beginning to feel that she really doesn't need my help as much as she needs the motivation.

Soon it's almost four o'clock and Mary Sue has actually finished all her math homework. I never would have thought this possible a few months ago.

"Mary Sue, doesn't it make you feel good to be finished and to know that you did almost all the problems by yourself?"

She tilts her head as she looks at me quizzically. "I wasn't thinking about how I feel, and even if you're right, I'd never admit it to *you.*"

"I know." I say, resigned to her ungrateful attitude, but glad I'm getting paid.

23. MORE SOFTBALL

The great feeling of having accomplished something with Mary Sue stays with me until the next gym class. I've finally gotten used to the idea that a softball isn't soft and it's really hard to catch, even with the right mitt on your hand. Today Miss Ditch actually expects us to hit the stupid ball with the bat. She demonstrates the ideal stance and swing. Nick pitches and Miss Ditch hits the ball into the outfield, making it look very easy. The girls line up, and most of them hit the ball when they are up at bat. I watch.

Yikes! It's my turn and guess who's behind me…Parsonfield. My hands are so sweaty, I can hardly hold the bat and my knees are shaking as I try to keep them bent. Nick pulls her right arm back holding the ball as if it's part of her hand. She makes a smooth arc with her arm and releases the ball. As it whizzes past, I swing the bat.

"Panic! You're not supposed to wait for the ball to go by and then swing!" Miss Ditch yells in my direction as Parsonfield laughs.

"Strike one," Nick says as she pitches me the next ball.

I see it coming toward me and I swing. Oops, that was too soon. The bat is pointing straight at Nick when the ball goes by.

"Strike two!" Parsonfield shouts loud enough to be heard through the brick walls of the whole school.

"Panic! Are you even *looking* at the ball? The idea is to hit it!" Miss Ditch's loud voice is a stabbing pain to my ears.

Nick looks at me and slowly pitches the ball right over the plate. I swing and miss.

"Strike three," Nick says just loud enough so everyone knows my turn is over.

I drop the bat on the ground, hang my head and pretend I'm a ladybug in the grass.

"Awright! Get outta my way, Pipsqueak!" Parsonfield growls as she grabs the bat on the ground.

Her stance is perfect. It's obvious she's done this before. I'll bet she played ball with the boys at the park. Nick pitches. The fast swish of the bat turns into a loud crack as it hits the ball. Wow! The ball sails off into the sky and lands in the far left field by the fence.

"Now, that's how it's done!" Miss Ditch shouts. "I hope you were all watching. Panic! Go get the ball. You can't do anything else right."

Why? Why does she always have to pick on me? I hate her. But now I'm glad for a chance to escape from Ditch, Parsonfield and the rest of the class. I run toward the spot where the ball went. The grass is almost up to my knees here and I am looking and looking, all along the fence. I look back trying to get some landmark or some idea whether to go right or left. I notice that the other girls are starting to head back to the locker room. Do I keep looking and risk being late for geometry? Or face Ditch without the ball? I keep pacing a little farther away from the fence. Ah, there's an uneven patch in the grass up ahead. Great, here it is! I snatch up the ball and turn to go back to the field. Everyone is long gone except Miss Ditch.

"It's about time you got your little butt back here," she says to me as I run back with the ball. "Hurry it up, you don't have time to shower or you'll be late for your next class. And I'm not wasting time writing you a pass either."

"Does that mean I don't get my point?"

"Of course not! I don't give points for retrieving balls. My dog can do that!"

Of course, only a gym teacher can be so mean and sarcastic! I bite my bottom lip, trying to keep the tears from my eyes. Miss Ditch just doesn't understand. I'm really trying in this stupid class, but she thinks I don't care and act dumb on purpose. I want to go up and shout in her face. I want to tell her that she's the meanest person in the whole world! I want to tell her that no one should be treated like she treats me. My mind is still telling her off as I get dressed and tie my ugly brown shoes. I hate my life. I want to scratch Josephine Btfsflk onto the bench. I want to know how to get rid of the black cloud.

I'm the only one left in the locker room. Better hurry. Miss Ditch is in her office, but I wouldn't even think of asking her for a late pass. Being late for geometry isn't the end of the world… getting Ditch permanently mad at me certainly is, because I need to pass gym.

I take a deep breath and leave for geometry class.

Over the next week, things don't get any better. Mary Sue manages to convince her Dad that she doesn't need my help anymore, so there goes my extra money. Miss Ditch is making my life totally miserable in gym class. She refuses to believe that a person really can't hit a softball. And then on Thursday, the worst happens. After another at bat and three more strikes, Miss Ditch yells "Is there anyone here who hasn't hit a softball yet? I mean, besides Panic?"

No one comes forward. All the girls shake their heads.

Parsonfield shouts "You oughta keep Panic after school, Miss Ditch, and tutor her. Lord knows, she needs it." Mary Sue smirks as she looks directly at me.

"Why can't you keep your mouth shut and mind your own business?" I mutter and glare at her.

"Great idea, Parsonfield!" Miss Ditch says enthusiastically.

I'm doomed. This *is* the end of the world. Staying after school…with Ditch. If there's such a thing as hell on earth, this is it. Maybe Mary Sue feels this way about algebra.

"Panic, come see me in my office after you get dressed."

When I stand in the doorway to her office, she looks up with an evil grin. Then, amazingly, her expression changes to one of pity.

Meet me here today, dressed to play at 3:05 sharp. Then we'll head to the field."

"Yes, Miss Ditch," I manage to respond weakly.

The entire day, the thought of just me and Ditch follows me like a dark cloud. I can barely pay attention to anyone or anything else.

I am almost relieved when the time comes. At least it will be over soon. I hurry to get dressed and at 3:04 I am standing in the doorway to Ditch's office.

She picks up a bat.

"Get the bucket of balls, Panic! And here's your motivation. For every hit you make, I'll give you ten points for your gym score. One more thing, we'll do this every day until you hit a softball."

I struggle with the bucket. It takes all the strength in my left arm to get it off the ground even an inch, and I have to use both hands. I hope Miss Ditch will help me.

Instead she says, "Not only are you uncoordinated, you're *weak*."

"I can't help it, Miss Ditch."

"You need some serious training, girl…boot camp."

My dad was a marine and he referred to boot camp as the worst time of his life—worse than starving in Poland and Germany before the war.

"Let's pick up the pace, girl."

I try to move as fast as I can to the field. If she really wants to get there, she should carry the bucket.

We finally make it to home plate where she hands me the bat. Effortlessly, Ditch picks up the bucket and carries it to the pitcher's mound.

"All right," she says. "Correct stance, knees bent, ready?"

She throws the first ball.

"Too slow."

Next.

"Too fast and too high."

Next.

"Too low."

"PANIC! Keep your eyes on the ball."

I am, but it's moving fast. I grit my teeth, squint my eyes and concentrate on the ball.

"Panic! You can't hit the ball if you don't swing!"

"Sorry, Miss Ditch" I mutter.

"Okay, let's try this again."

"Too fast! Panic, can you SEE the ball? I mean, you are swinging as if you don't even see it."

"Of course I can see. I don't need glasses. When the nurse gives us eye tests every year I always get 20-20," I say in a firm voice, looking straight at her.

Miss Ditch finally checks her watch and sighs.

"It's almost four o'clock. You better head to the locker room and get changed. I don't want you to miss the late bus. And don't forget. Tomorrow, same time, same place…until you hit a softball."

Every muscle in my stiff, tense body finally relaxes. Miss Ditch takes the ball bucket back to the locker room, and I hurry to get dressed, get my stuff and make it to the late bus.

Stepping up on the bus, I see Tom and manage a weak smile.

"Hi! Pardon my saying this, but you look like you've been fighting your way through a wind tunnel. Rough day of tutoring?" Tom asks.

"No."

I don't want to tell him that I'm the klutz of the century…probably the only kid in the history of the world who's been kept after school 'cause she couldn't hit a softball.

"Well, we're not a person of many words today, are we?"

"No, I mean…oh, you wouldn't believe why I've been after school anyway."

"Try me."

"Okay. It was for gym."

"What? Did you say gym?"

"Yeah. I can't hit a softball."

"Are you *serious*? You just watch it coming and swing the bat when it's almost over the plate. A gym teacher *really* kept you after school for that?"

"Yes."

Tom laughs. "Sorry, but that's the funniest thing I've heard in a long time. Oh, it's my stop. Will I see you tomorrow?"

"Afraid so."

No, that's not what I meant, I hope he didn't hear my answer. I do want to see him tomorrow. Why can't I even carry on a decent conversation? I am such a loser. I always say the wrong thing.

Soon I get off the bus and trudge home.

I wish I could just skip high school and go to college. The road seems longer than ever and the hill steeper than I remember.

Maybe there's a cave inside the hill. I imagine a secret rock and if I say "Open Sesame" it will let me into the cave where I can hide never to see Miss Ditch or Parsonfield again. That Mary Sue! She had to suggest to Ditch that she *tutor* me. She's still the same mean brat she was when we lived next door on Waltz Way before we moved to the country.

#

Almost a half an hour later I get home. Annie is waiting at the cellar door.

"I've been so worried about you. Good grief, you look absolutely exhausted. I heard a rumor that Miss Ditch kept you after school."

"Yes, I've been in hell with Miss Ditch."

"What? Why? Tell me."

"For the last two weeks we've been doing softball in gym, and I'm the only one who never hit the ball. I wish I was blind!"

"Kennie, you can't mean that," Annie says.

"I do. Because no one expects a blind person to hit a softball! Remember that nice lady who lived downstairs from us in the apartment when we were real little? Mom told us that she could hear every little sound because she was blind; so we had to put our slippers on when we came in the door. She used to get around her apartment without ever bumping into the furniture or anything. She cooked, and even fell in love and got married."

"Oh, Kennie, you really don't know what she went through, and I'll bet a lot of it was worse than Miss Ditch's class."

"It's not just in class now. That nasty, pain-in-the-butt Parsonfield gave Ditch the idea to *tutor* me. It would be different if I really wasn't trying. But the harder I try, the harder it is. I just can't do it. I *hate* it. I *hate* who I am. Why can't I be normal and do the simple things like everybody else can? Maybe my brain got disconnected from my muscles when I fell off Mary Sue's swing a long time ago." I start to cry.

Annie puts her arm around my shoulder.

"It's okay. This can't go on forever. Either you'll hit it or Ditch will give up."

"Not likely." I say. I really can't do it, and Ditch is the most persistent person in the universe," I say between sniffles.

"It'll be all right," says Annie. "You just can't let Ditch and a softball take over your whole life. There's the Leprechaun, and "A"s in your other classes. Think about how much you like art class, and how good your drawings are."

24. THE CHEERING SQUAD

Day after day, I try to follow Annie's advice. The sessions with Miss Ditch continue.

'Too high... too low... too fast... too slow... keep your eye on the ball' echo in my brain like a haunting tune that just won't stop. We've been doing this for eight days now. Miss Ditch insists I can do it, I try and try and still the bat never touches the ball. Why is this so impossible? How come everyone in the world can do this? Is it because I don't believe or because something is wrong with my brain? Could I have some connections that don't work fast? Maybe I have stuffed too much math and other things in my head and now my brain can't talk to my muscles like normal people's brain cells do. It's about more than just hitting a ball. Think about those stupid coordination exercises. This is the mystery that haunts my life. It isn't a simple matter of not trying hard enough, like Miss Ditch thinks. There has to be a logical explanation for this. It's more than effort and attitude.

Day nine, here in the locker room, the only sounds are the echoes in my head of "too fast...too slow and on and on". Maybe this will be the day Miss Ditch gives up. One can always hope.

At 3:05 on the dot, Miss Ditch appears with a bat in one hand and the bucket in the other.

"Are you ready to go, Panic? Is this going to be the day you hit it?"

"I hope so."

She has no idea how much I truly hope so! She hands me the bat as we walk silently to the field. No two human beings could possibly be more opposite. But we both want the same thing, for this bat in my hand to hit a moving ball.

Miss Ditch takes her position on the mound. I grasp the bat with both hands, hold it up over my right shoulder, look down at the exact position of my feet and bend my knees.

Almost as if reading my mind, Miss Ditch says, "Good stance, Panic. Take a few practice swings."

As I move, the bat swishes through the air.

"Looks good," she says. That's what you want to do when the ball comes. Just keep your eye on it. Ready?"

"Yep."

She releases the ball, the bat swishes, but the ball keeps on going to the backstop.

"Close, but too fast."

Again and again we repeat the motions. The ball always flies past me.

The sound of laughter and chatter breaks the monotony. I look up and there by the fence is a group of kids. My heart stops. It's Mary Sue, Vicki, their friends and a bunch of guys with cigarettes in their hands.

"Hi! Panic! We came to cheer you on!"

"Yeah, Pancake, you can do it! Hit the ball to us! We'll catch it! HaHa!"

"Go Panic! Go."

"As they say in theater, 'break a leg'!"

"Break the bat!"

No one deserves this harassment. Isn't torture from Ditch enough? Now, them!

"Panic, you show them. You can do this! Ready?"

If ever I wanted a wish to come true, it's now. I want to hit that ball so hard it knocks one of their heads off.

I grit my teeth and I squeeze the bat, my murder weapon. I concentrate on the ball as it's coming; I picture the arc and position the bat just a little higher. For a split second the ball disappears. Then I swing with every muscle in my body and every ounce of strength I can muster.

The ball flies past the bat an instant too soon. It's as if it had a mind of its own and picked up speed at the last second. The bat continues to pull me around with it and I land in a heap on the ground.

The guffaws and shouts from the fence are unbearable.

I don't even want to see Ditch's face. Can I die now?

"Y'all get out of here!" Miss Ditch shouts to the gang at the fence.

"C'mon, let's go," Mary Sue says just loud enough for me to hear.

I look up enough to see them slowly drifting away toward the building.

"Okay, Panic. You need a change of pace. Get up and run a lap or two around the track."

I get up and dust myself off. Leaving the bat on the ground, I start to run and run. This almost feels good as my feet make their own rhythm ..baap.... baap.... baap.... baap.... baap.... baap.... baap.... Faster and faster, the sound drowns out the "too slow, too fast..." tune. I keep going. The breeze on my face gets stronger and pulls on my ponytail. I'm all alone, suspended in this strange world of sunshine, blue sky, wind and ground beneath my feet. There is no time or limits to the space.

"Panic! PANIC! PANIC! You can stop now!"

Miss Ditch's shouts yank me back to the other world. I slow down and finally stop. Sweat drips from my forehead, my armpits are drenched and I smell like the locker room at the end of the day.

Miss Ditch comes over to me. Is that a smile I see on her face? "Panic! That was amazing!" she says. "Do you have any idea how fast you can run?"

Me? Amazing? Did Miss Ditch really say that?

"No," I tell her. "Why? Did you think I was fast?"

"Sure seemed like it. Tomorrow, after you hit a ball, I'll bring my stopwatch and time you. But you better hurry or you'll miss the late bus."

I run to the locker room, leaving her with the bat and bucket of balls. I need a shower...but it's almost four o'clock. I pull off the sweaty gym suit and stuff it in my bag. It's got to be washed before tomorrow. I put on my blouse and skirt. My slip, socks and shoes go in the bag with the gym suit. I'll just wear my gym shoes home. Miss Ditch is coming in from the field as I race down the hall.

"Bye, Panic! I'll see you tomorrow." She shouts after me.

"Okay, Bye!" I shout back, glancing over my shoulder.

I barely make it to the bus.

"Where have you been? Looks like you ran all the way from Timbuktu!" the driver says, trying to be friendly.

I look around for an empty seat, and Tom smiles and raises his hand to get my attention. Now is not the time to sit next to him. I smell like locker room sweat, my hair is falling out of my ponytail, and my clothes are a mess. I pretend that I just don't notice him as I look down shuffling my stuff in my arms. I head to the back of the bus and sit as far away from everyone as I can. I plop in the seat as exhaustion overwhelms me.

25. CAUGHT BETWEEN TWO SOFTBALLS

When the sunlight shines through our white curtains, I know it's time to get up. Every part of me aches. I try to move, but it's like my body is embedded in cement. Why can't it be Saturday? I manage to get one foot out from under the covers and finally both of them are on the floor. Annie is already dressed and putting on her socks.

"You better move a lot faster than that if we're going to catch the bus. I can't believe you slept this long."

I push myself to move and wish I had time to take a long hot shower.

A face stares at me from the bathroom mirror, looking like some zombie with circles under the eyes, ratty hair sticking out all over, and a furrowed brow as if in pain. Too bad it's not Halloween. I tell myself to hurry up, and not to forget the blue gym suit I'd left hanging on the line to dry in the laundry room. I go through the motions, but my mind is miles away, trying to ignore the pain.

When I put the toothpaste back on the shelf in the medicine cabinet, I spy the Ben-Gay. That's what Dad uses when he's been working too hard outside. It's supposed to make sore muscles feel better. I stand on tiptoe to reach it. That top shelf is just a bit too high, so I use the back of my toothbrush to nudge it towards me. Oops, too much. The Ben-Gay goes flying…right into the toilet.

No! no choice but to put your hand in and pull it out, yuck!

I retrieve it like a dead fish and drop it into the sink, run the water and make soapsuds to clean the wrinkled metal tube and my hands. I try and try and finally the cap twists off. It doesn't smell good, but if it helps the muscles, it'll be worth it. I rub the white creamy stuff on my legs where it hurts most, then my shoulders. It feels tingly and warm. It really seems to help.

"Keeennniiieee, I need to use the potty!" Bonnie screams as she pounds on the door with her fists.

Quickly I screw the cap back on the Ben-Gay and put it on the shelf in the medicine cabinet.

When I open the door, Bonnie pinches her nose. "Pee-yew. It's smells really bad in here!"

I dash out of the bathroom so I don't have to talk to her. I finish my cereal as fast as I can and hurry downstairs to get my gym suit. It's still a little damp, but I pull it off the line and stuff it into my bag. It's wrinkled anyway.

I hear Bonnie's voice in the kitchen complaining. "No, Mommy. It's not poo. It's worse!"

Uh, oh, I've really got to get out of here, and fast. The last thing I need now is a battle with Bratty Bonnie. Where's Annie?

As if on cue, Annie calls down the stairs "Hey, Kennie are you ready?"

"Almost!"

After putting my shoes on, I get up from the floor slowly even though my muscles don't hurt as much as they did before the Ben-Gay.

When Annie gets downstairs, she asks, "Kennie, what is that smell? It reminds me of that cream stuff Dad uses."

"Yeah, it is. My muscles ache so much. I guess they're stiff from running yesterday. It's weird because it makes your skin warm, but it does help a lot."

"I'm glad it helps, but it *really* smells bad," Annie says.

"Do you think I can wash it off in the laundry sink down here?" I ask.

"Afraid there's no time for that; we'll miss the bus. Besides I think it'll take a good shower with plenty of soap to get rid of that smell." Annie says. "Let's get going."

A cool breeze blows in our faces as we open the cellar door. Maybe this will help get rid of the smell while we walk to the bus stop.

The bus pulls up just as we get there. Going down the aisle to an empty seat heads turn and kids sniff the air curiously. There ought to be a warning on the Ben-Gay tube: "This cream will stink up any space the user is in." I'm almost glad I have gym first today so I can shower and get rid of the smell. I must be getting used to it, but it is pretty strong.

"No, it's not B.O." I hear someone say.

They are talking about me. *Can I trade my life for anyone else's?*

When the bus stops in front of the school, I wait until everyone else gets off.

“Cheez, kid, you smell like a chemistry lab!” The bus driver says. “I guess it could be worse. Good luck today.”

I’ll need it. I am extra careful going down the steps of the bus. Tripping is not on my schedule.

By the time I get to homeroom, I have already had a million strange stares and unwanted comments. I sit by the window instead of my usual seat. Parsonfield spots me instantly.

“Panic, you’re not sitting in your seat? Why?” she bellows and she saunters across the front of the room.

“We don’t have assigned seats in here.” I answer, wanting to add and it’s none of her business.

“Ewww! Blech! You smell like an old person in a nursing home!” Parsonfield announces to the whole room.

I look down and I feel my face turning red.

Do I have to start my day with her? I wonder if you can switch homerooms. But, I wouldn’t want to lose the Leprechaun. Could I get her moved? Why can’t I just stand up to her?

When I get to the crowded locker room, girls step back as I approach, breathing out and waving a hand in front of their faces. I take out my gym suit. It’s wrinkled a lot worse than I thought, but I put it on anyway.

Parsonfield waits until the locker room is abuzz and then stands up on a bench to be sure she’s heard.

“Ladies, we have a problem in here. It’s this awful smell! It seems that Panic has decided that she is not only dumb, stupid and uncoordinated, but now she has to pretend to be an old person and grace us with this dreadful smell of ‘eau de nursing home’. What do you say we throw her out of here?”

All eyes turn on me. I shiver. Parsonfield steps toward me still walking on the bench; she really towers over me now. I bite my lip and turn to race out into the hall. I get to the doorway and almost run into Miss Ditch.

"Going the wrong way, aren't you, Panic?"

I freeze and say nothing. Trapped.

She reaches her arm out and turns me around. The first thing she sees in the chaos of the locker room is Parsonfield standing on the bench.

"I demand to know what's going on here! Let's start with you, Parsonfield. What are you doing up there?"

"I had something important to say," Mary Sue answers. "We have a situation that needs to be dealt with."

Miss Ditch frowns. "I am the one who deals with situations in here. Now, why don't you tell me what this situation is?"

"Well, it's kinda obvious," says Mary Sue rolling her eyes at me. "We have all been insulted."

"How?" asks Miss Ditch, "by whom?"

"Panic and her ugly, smelly, stupid self."

Miss Ditch looks at her and then at me. I am sure she is clueless.

"I am in charge of this class. I will not tolerate this nonsense. Now, Parsonfield, get off that bench and the rest of you…out on the field."

My fear of the wrath of Miss Ditch subsides, as I go outside. The fresh air helps, too. I can't wait until we are done with softball. I never knew anyone could hate a sport as much as I do. We do more of the usual exercises. I am now only one count behind most of the time and I do think I'm a bit stronger in doing "girl-push ups" from the knees. This morning it's hard to do almost everything with my aching muscles. I am so tired. I wish I could disappear into the tall grass and take a nap.

Miss Ditch seems to sense that I am a mess and she doesn't even comment on my wrinkled gym suit or the circles under my eyes.

As Nick and Mason pick teams, Parsonfield is being her usual self.

"Miss Ditch! That ain't fair. I'm a much better player than Mason. I should be the Captain! How can you choose her to pick a team?"

"Parsonfield, it's more than skill that counts when you're a Captain. Attitude and sportsmanship are a lot more important, and I'm not impressed with yours this morning."

"Well, it's all Panic's fault! Look at that pitiful pipsqueak. She comes in smelling gross, can't even hit a ball, is so stupid she can't do coordination exercises after all these months, and you expect us to *like* her!?"

"Parsonfield, it's not a matter of liking her, or anyone else. You have to be part of a team, and as a captain you especially need to set a good example. You have to be fair and play together. Acting like a bully is not acceptable. You take your place on a team and play the game by the rules. I don't want any more petty nonsense out of you."

Of course, I am one of the 'left-overs' after each of the teams has nine players, two coaches and a scorekeeper.

Miss Ditch turns to us "Okay, you five go to the far outfield and practice. Start with a small circle and as you each catch the softball once, then make the circle bigger." She throws me a ball, which I miss.

Miss Ditch just shakes her head.

So here we are the five outcasts, like lepers sent as far away as possible from the village. *But it's not like clumsiness is a disease that's contagious. What is it anyway? Can it be inherited? Not likely, both my parents and my sisters are athletically normal and very coordinated. Mom was a dancer and Dad a swimmer and a diver.*

Oops, I should be paying attention; the ball just whizzed past me. I turn to search for it in the tall grass. The other four girls just stand there for a bit.

"Oh, look! I found a four-leaf clover!" I shout ecstatically.

The other girls rush over and admire my treasure, until one says, "we'll have no luck if we don't find this ball soon."

With the softball lost in the grass, we have become comrades in a search party.

There's no one to tease us out here. No shouts from the lovely Miss Ditch. This isn't so bad.

One member of our party decides to desert us and go back to get another ball. We four keep looking. I slip the four-leaf clover in my belt and tighten it. This beats playing catch any day. Our *Deserter* returns with a ball.

"Girls please don't lose this one. We have already angered the Ditch, and I'm not one to be going back there one minute sooner than I have to. We better let her see us throwing this stupid thing or she'll get on our case."

If we were native Americans, we would all have names that describe us. Now I think, hers would be *Brave One* rather than *Deserter*.

As we form our circle again, there are only four of us. *Brave One* reaches up with her right arm and throws the *grapefruit* in my direction. I am watching it carefully as it is caught by the wind and comes sailing toward me. Just as I reach up to catch it, I see another ball heading straight for my face. One hits me on the left cheek and the other manages to hit the fingers of my right hand so hard they bend backwards. I want to scream, but fear of the Ditch arriving in 'Outcast Village' makes me hold my breath. My four comrades gather around me, trying to comfort me. I hold my tingling fingers with my left hand, wishing for some ice to numb the pain. At least there's some feeling in them. I hope my face doesn't turn all black and blue.

A whistle blows. Miss Ditch shouts as loudly as the shrill whistle. "Now, what's your excuse for not practicing up there? I should have known better than to let Panic out of my sight!"

Oh please just leave us alone here in "Outcast Village." But somehow I know we are all in deep cow dung with the Ditch. In a matter of moments, our nice village will be dissolved.

Sure enough, Ditch is storming up the hill toward us.

I don't know which is worse: pain or fear.

"Panic! What happened now?"

"Miss Ditch, it wasn't really her fault," *Brave One* volunteers. " You see, just as I came back with another ball

Lyman found the first one and we both threw them at Panic at the same time. She couldn't possibly catch them both. No one could."

"So, are you hurt?" Ditch demands glaring at me.

"Well her face isn't very pretty, it's getting red and look at how her fingers are starting to swell up," *Brave One* replies.

"Can't she even speak for herself?"

"Umm, yeah."

"Well if you can walk, just go to the nurse's office. I better not take any more chances with you. BUT I will see you at 3:05 sharp this afternoon! Lyman, you go with her. The rest of you, get that ball moving in the air!"

We try to hurry down the hill, past the softball field and back into the building.

"Look! Look! Pipsqeak Panic got hurt!" Parsonfield has to be sure everyone knows I'm a mess …again. I look straight at her and make a fist.

26. THE NURSE'S OFFICE

"Let's stop in the locker room to get your stuff; I don't think the nurse will want you to come back here," Linda Lyman says.

I try to open my locker but I just can't hold the dial so I use my left hand while Linda holds the lock still. I struggle with it and finally it pops open. My face is starting to burn and I can't wait to get out of here. Linda helps get my stuff out and carries my books.

As we walk down the hall, some tall kid stops his long strides and grimaces. He asks me, "Man, who beat you up?"

Linda says, "Whitey Ball." And hurries me along.

"Whitey who?" I ask.

"You know—Whitey, as in white. Ball, as in softball."

I smile a little. "Clever answer, how'd you manage to think of that so quickly?"

"I have three brothers and you have to be quick with the quips or they really get to you. I've had a lot of practice."

When we get to the nurse's office, Linda sets my stuff down and says, "Good luck with everything."

Then I remember the four-leaf clover. I loosen my belt, take the clover out and give it to Linda.

"Cool, thanks. I've never found one of these," she says placing it carefully in the palm of her hand.

"You're welcome. And thanks for introducing me to Whitey Ball."

As Linda leaves, the nurse comes in and says "Aren't you the one who had the horrible nosebleed last fall?"

"Yes, Ma'am. But I was hoping you'd forgotten me by now."

"What happened? Gym class again?" Mrs. McNight asks.

"Yes, I was the victim of two softballs being thrown at me at once. In case no one's ever told you, softballs are *not soft*!"

"Right you are about that. Let's get some ice on this face before it swells up too much." She goes to the small fridge and pulls out an ice pack.

As I reach for it with my right hand, she says, "Oh dear, look at those fingers! It's a good thing you don't have a ring on. This hand looks badly bruised, but not likely that there's anything broken. How did this happen?"

"When I tried to catch the other ball, it hit my hand funny and bent my fingers back."

"This calls for an ice bath," she says as she goes back to the freezer and pulls out two ice cube trays.

"Dear, by the look on your face you'd think this was a torture chamber. Just relax. I'm going to put this ice in a small basin with water for you to soak your hand in. That's all."

Boy, am I glad I'm the only one in here. The bell rings. I should be going to geometry. The Captain will be okay with me being late and besides I'll have a pass from the nurse. I exhale and start to relax. I can't believe how tired I feel, and it's only second period. My head nods and Mrs. McNight taps me on the shoulder.

"Would you like to lie down on the cot? It looks like you could use some rest, Kenda."

"Huh? Umm, no I don't want to sleep I need to look at my French again for my test third period," I say with a shiver.

"Kenda, I wish the students who visit me on a regular basis were half as conscientious as you are. Most kids come in here to try to get out of tests," the nurse says. "Sure you don't want to lie down?"

"I guess a short nap will be okay."

Slowly I walk over to the cot and lie down; it does feel good to rest my tired body. I cross my arms above my waist and rub them with my hands to try to get rid of the goose bumps. Mrs. McNight can tell that I'm freezing. She brings a white thermal blanket to me and gently lays it over my chest and arms and it covers my knees and calves as well.

The time passes and soon the nurse tells me to sit up and see if I feel up to going to the cafeteria.

"I think I can," I say.

But then I don't really want to face Mary Sue and Vicki's gang.

"Do I have to?"

"All right, why don't you tell me the rest of the story?" Mrs. McKnight asks kindly.

"There isn't any more."

"Surely, you feel self-conscious going to lunch with that bruise on your face? Are there kids who tease you?"

How does she know? Hmm, maybe I can strike a deal with her.

"If I tell you, will you let me eat my lunch here?"

"Well, I don't usually let students stay here for lunch… but I suppose, I could make an exception for you."

"Thanks."

"Did you bring your lunch?"

"We always buy lunch." I answer.

"Erik will be here for his medicine in a few minutes, I'll ask him to get your lunch for you," Mrs. McNight says.

As the door opens, Erik says, "Mrs. McNight, I'm here for my medicine." Then he stops and looks at me through his thick glasses. His eyes seem really big. *Is that the lenses or an expression of surprise?*

"Erik, as usual, you are right on time. I could set my watch by you," Mrs.McNight says. "After you take your pill, could you do me a big favor?"

"Sure."

"I need you to buy a lunch and bring it back here for Kenda," she says handing him lunch money.

"Of course," he says as he looks at me and the corners of his mouth turn up just a bit. He takes the coins from the nurse, turns and goes out the door.

"Okay, now Miss Kenda. Let's hear the rest of the story."

"Well, you see, when we were little, Mary Sue Parsonfield lived next door. I think she was born bossy and always treated me and her little brother like babies. Then one day I fell off her swing and our mothers paid attention to me and not her. She hated that. She never wanted to let me play, but she always liked my big sister, Annie."

"You'd think she would have forgotten all that by now," Mrs. McNight says.

"Yeah," I continue. "Now she's part of the gang that smokes and hangs out in the girl's bathroom across from the cafeteria. Vicki, 'Queen Victoria', is the gang-leader. Vicki threatened me once, and Mary Sue never loses a chance to be mean to me in our homeroom and gym class. Miss Ditch likes her 'cause she's athletic and I'm horrible. Of course, with a name like Pannek, I am always laughed at. Now, Mary Sue and the rest of them try to trap me near the cafeteria. I avoid them at all cost and Mrs. Anders lets me use the bathroom by her room before I go to lunch. Today, I know they are waiting for me, because Mary Sue saw my face before I came here. She feels like a big cheese and gets points with Vicki whenever she uses me for their entertainment. That's the story."

"So what are you going to do about it?" Mrs. McNight asks.

"Just ignore her and the whole bunch and keep away from them. What else can I do?" I say.

"You could tell her to stop it. You don't have to let her give you a hard time," the nurse says.

"Easy for you to say," I reply.

Then I realize Erik is standing in the doorway with my tray.

"She's right, Kenda," he says. "It's like my Mom tells me 'Don't let anybody down you.'"

"Huh? Erik! You have no room to talk! I think you're a big wimp." I tell him.

"That's good! That's the idea, Kenda," Erik says nodding his head.

"Yeah, but I'm talking to *you*, not Mary Sue or Vicki," I reply. "Besides, when have *you* ever stood up to her?"

"When I told her to 'get out of my way' last week and when I refused to let her have my seat by the door in homeroom on the first day of school. Then there was the time I tripped Vicki. They can think whatever they want about me, 'cause I know who I am. They don't call me names or give me a hard time to my face," Erik explains.

"Hmm, I think you're right. I've never seen them taunt you like they do me," I say.

"You're right, Erik," Mrs. McNight says taking the tray from him, "I couldn't have told her better myself. Thank you for getting Kenda's lunch. Now let me write you a pass for your next class."

He looks back over his shoulder and the corners of his mouth turn up, ever so slightly. As Erik leaves, he says, "Okay, Bye."

"Oh! Mrs. McNight, I better hurry and finish my lunch so I can get dressed for Art class." My right hand hurts, so I'm holding my pizza in my left hand.

"You have time, Kenda," she says.

When I finish eating my lunch with my left hand, I rustle through my stuff, pull out my clothes and get dressed.

"Bye, Mrs. McNight," I say as I walk out the door.

"Think about what Erik told you, and have a good weekend," the nurse says. "With a little luck you'll be good as new by Monday."

My art teacher raises his eyebrow and pulls on his mustache with his thumb and index finger when I walk in the room. It's almost as if he wants to say something, but doesn't know what.

Margy speaks out for everyone. "Holy cow! Kenda! What happened to you? I can't imagine *you* getting into a fight!"

"On no, not a real fight, I just got caught between two flying softballs."

The teacher says, "This is a great opportunity for us to think about showing motion in our drawings."

He proceeds to sketch some examples of a flying ball, a cartoon bird, and a racecar on the board. He is absolutely amazing. To come up with these things and draw them really well and fast blows me away.

With a sepia-colored pastel in my hand, I try to think of anything BUT a ball that I can draw. I've seen enough airplanes take off and land at the airport where Dad works, but it's hard to picture them moving. It's almost like they just change positions against the sky and clouds. When the teacher comes over, he notices my swollen, bluish hand.

"Kenda, if you'd like to take this home over the weekend and bring it in on Monday, that'll be fine. It doesn't look like that hand is in any shape to draw."

"Thanks," I whisper, grateful that he doesn't make a big deal of it.

I watch Renee and Margy hard at work on their sketches. Margy has such natural talent, she's fun to watch.

Soon the bell rings and I head for English class.

27. TRAPPED AGAIN

As I get to the stairs, Mary Sue and the whole mean gang are blocking my way. Mary Sue points at me.

"There's the stupid Pipsqueak! See I told you she can't even catch a ball. You need some make-up real bad, girl!"

"Naha, she'd really look dumb, like a seven year-old playing dress-up," one of the others chimes in.

Vicki grins and laughs.

"Hah! Yeah! That was some pretty cool trick conning the nurse into lettin' you stay there through three classes. And then we know who brought you lunch…don't we, girls?"

"Yeah, boyfriend, Erik!" Mary Sue answers.

"The dummy with the thick glasses and crooked teeth," another girl adds.

"Haha! The ugly one."

"Don't you talk mean about him!" I say, holding my shoulders back and standing up tall.

"Don't you talk mean about him." Mary Sue mimics me and imitates my stance.

"He can't help how he looks and he's a lot nicer than any of you," I say to Mary Sue's face.

"Since when are you standing up for him?" she asks. "He *must* be your boyfriend."

Vicki and the others continue to taunt me. I try to duck to the right and around the stair railing. But Rod sticks out his arm and leg and I almost trip on the step. I grab the handrail as if hanging on for dear life. I bite my bottom lip to keep from crying. I don't believe in God anymore. If there was a good God he wouldn't put people like Vicki and Mary Sue on earth to torture me.

"Break it up here! Vhat's goink on?" Mr. Zolnerovich, the Russian teacher asks. The football coach is right behind him.

"Do I need to escort some bodies to the office?" the coach bellows.

They all scatter.

"Are zhey tryink to geef you a hart time?" Mr. Z asks me.

"I'm okay now. Thanks," I say as I hurry on to English class.

Mrs. Anders says nothing, although I'm sure she sees the mess my face is in.

I want this whole day to be over. English class is okay, and Mrs. Anders won't let the kids be rude in here. Today we are discussing the importance of dialogue in a novel. Some students raise their hands with examples. But too many are chatting among themselves and not paying attention to the classmate speaking. Mrs. Anders decides it's time to change seats, and break up the cliques. She quickly calls names and seats kids alphabetically one aisle at a time, from the front to the back. I end up in the very last seat in the third aisle. At the end of class, she writes our homework on the board. I squint, but I still can't read it. So I ask Sharon what it says.

I scribble down the homework and plan a route to the gym that will avoid Vicki's gang. I wonder what would happen if I just don't show up. The wrath of Ditch…no, I don't even want to think about it.

28. TRACK

When the bell rings, I go around the back hallway upstairs, then come downstairs on the other side of the building from the cafeteria. I peer around the corner of the hallway at the bottom. Coast is clear. Quickly I make a dash for the locker room.

Whew. Safe again, just me and the four walls and a lot of empty lockers.

Do I hear voices? I tiptoe closer to Miss Ditch's office and hear her talking. "Now I can begin to understand what my physical therapist did for me. After the accident that left me paralyzed, she pushed me to the limit over and over. I had no idea how hard it was to be tough and demanding, and how frustrating it is to see so little progress with some kids. The girls just think I'm mean. But I want them all to feel the kind of satisfaction I did when I took that first step. They need to be pushed until they succeed. Don't you think?"

"To an extent, but you are trying too hard to make athletes out of them all. There are some kids who are born clumsy, and you shouldn't worry about them."

Miss Ditch starts talking again, "It's not about making them athletes as much as it is making them realize they can stand up to challenges, and win. I believe that if a girl with no confidence and a totally passive personality can take that first step, she'll learn to take challenges head-on."

Could she be talking about me? I better sneak over to my locker before she knows I'm here. The lock is open. Renee must have left it that way. I'm glad, I don't want to try to open it with my aching hand. I just realize that I've had my gym shoes on all day, nice. I don't have to tie any shoes either. So I just put my gym suit back on and I decide that snaps are easier than buttons. The belt is a challenge, but I manage to get it together.

Another gym teacher comes out of the office followed by Miss Ditch.

"Panic! Are you alive?" Miss Ditch asks.

"Yes, Ma'am, but I'm not sure I can even hold a bat, no less hit a softball."

"That's all right."

Am I dreaming? What did she say?

"Miss Ditch, did you say it's all right that I don't have to try to hit a softball today?"

"Yes. You heard me! I have given up on you and softball…on you and coordination exercises. …But, I do want you to stay."

"What? I mean, Why?"

"Panic! I want to know how fast you can run," Miss Ditch answers. "We're heading out to the track, and I've got my stopwatch."

Good thing I rested in the nurse's office. I'm going to need all the energy I can muster. But, man, am I glad I don't have to keep my eye on those stupid balls coming at me.

So here we are out on the track, just the two of us, Miss Ditch and me. Strange, I almost feel okay with this. I go to the line on the inside lane.

"Do you want to do a few stretches and warm ups?" she asks.

"Okay, if I can keep them simple."

I start to do plain old two-position jumping jacks. As I move, the muscle aches return.

How could I forget the pain from yesterday? Maybe it's like they say: it feels good when you stop hitting your head against the wall.

I stop and stretch, right leg out, arms over; left leg out, arms over; repeat again and again. Then hands on hips, twist at the waist right, left, right, left.

"How about some lunges?"

So I do these: right, left, right, left, and repeat the sequence again. Ouch, those calf muscles are stiff! Then I glance back at Miss Ditch.

Standing to the side of the track, with her thumb on the button of her stopwatch. "Okay?" she calls to me. "Ready, set, go!"

I take off running. Not too fast at first, but then my feet start to get into their rhythm. A little faster I tell myself, and I sense my body going faster and my ponytail swishing as I move with the breeze on my face. I keep running in my own world not even realizing that I passed the line already.

"Panic! You can stop now. Hmm…not too shabby, 7.35 minutes," Miss Ditch says nodding her head.

"See if you can do it again."

Man, I'm tired, but this sure beats softball. I go back to the starting line.

"Ready, set, go!"

I take off faster this time, and keep on going. The breeze on my face feels stronger, and I can feel the bruise smarting.

Run, Kenda, run. Run faster, I tell myself. My feet sound out their comfortable rhythm, baap… baap… baap… baap… The world doesn't exist, only the sky, the wind, and the track beneath my feet. It's like I'm suspended in time and space, only vaguely aware that I'm running.

"Panic!" the voice of Miss Ditch suddenly brings me back to earth.

"That was great! 7.18 minutes."

"Again. …. Ready, set, go"

Again I run and run. It feels great, until a sudden pain in my calf almost makes me fall. It's like an invisible dog is biting on the back of my right leg. Ouch! I reach down and the muscle is hard as a rock. I sit down on the track and rub it.

"Panic! Got a charley horse? Or did you fall?" Miss Ditch shouts from the opposite side of the track.

As I sit and rub my leg, it starts to feel a little better. In no time at all, Miss Ditch is standing beside me.

"Looks like a classic charley horse. Better call it quits for today. You may never hit a softball, but you've got potential as a runner."

I'm not sure what to say, as Miss Ditch helps me up. I have never felt so exhausted in my life, but I'm happy, very happy.

"You know, Panic, life is full of lessons. Sometimes we learn them in the strangest ways, and not always in the classroom. Sometimes the teacher learns more than the student."

We slowly make our way back to the building and Miss Ditch leaves me in the locker room. I change back into my school clothes and go to Miss Ditch's office to say goodbye. She's on the phone.

"Yes, Yes! I did say Panic! I never would have believed it either!" Her excited voice carries through the closed door. This is a good thing I say to myself, something not to be interrupted. So I quietly leave the locker room, walk down the empty halls and out in the sunshine, smiling. What a crazy day!

#

"I think I need glasses," I announce at the dinner table.

"Why?" Mom asks.

"My new seat is in the very back of the room in English class," I say, "and I can't see the board."

Dad looks at Mom.

"Well, I'll call my eye doctor tomorrow," Mom says, "and see how soon he can check your eyes."

29. THE TEAM

On Thursday, I bounce of out of bed and race to the bathroom so I can be first. I shower and get dressed. This is the first day I've really been happy to be going to high school. I finally feel like I belong. Yeah my face still looks awful, but it's not for life. The bluish purple color is turning a greenish yellow and it will clear up.

In homeroom, Mary Sue can't wait to be sure the class knows about my latest softball disaster.

"Hey, y'all look at Panic!" she announces the minute her feet are in the door. "She messed up her face in gym class. Stupid little klutz! She'll tell you all about it."

I'm not going to let her ruin my day.

I speak out, surprising even myself. "Actually I was attacked by Whitey Ball."

The whole class and the Leprechaun look at me, startled and begin to laugh. I do too. It sounds so ridiculous, it's funny.

Everyone is laughing except Mary Sue. She narrows her eyes at me and says something else. But she can't be heard over the chatter and chuckles.

"Looks like you took the wind out of her sails," Mr. LeCourt says in a whisper leaning toward me.

As I head out the door, Erik gives me a thumbs-up and I smile.

"I'll get even with you in gym, just you wait," Mary Sue threatens, as she steps up beside me.

I ignore her. She doesn't know what happened after school.

When we get to the locker room, I just get my locker open when Mary Sue slams it.

"Hey! What did you do that for? That's my locker too!" Renee shouts in her face.

Parsonfield takes two steps back, but doesn't reply.

"Hey, are you sure you're okay? Looks like your face got pretty messed up from that softball," Renee says.

"It's okay and doesn't hurt any more—just looks bad."

When we get out on the field, Miss Ditch doesn't make us do any eight-step coordination exercises, and she tells us to all take a partner. Renee is mine.

"Looks like we have an odd number. Mason you can be Renee's partner," Miss Ditch says. "Panic! Come with me."

"What?" I ask.

"We all know how you'd do on this softball test, so I'd rather have you see if you can run a mile in less than seven minutes instead," Miss Ditch says, pulling the stopwatch out of her pocket.

"Who are you kidding, Miss Ditch?! That ain't fair! Everyone *has* to take the skills test." Parsonfield objects, practically in Miss Ditch's face.

"Excuse me, Parsonfield. YOU do NOT make the rules in here. Is that clear? Get over there with your partner and get started," Miss Ditch commands.

Parsonfield turns and walks away, looking down at the ground.

I am off and running, my feet getting into their rhythm, my whole spirit soaring.

"Panic! You can stop now. That was fast, but not quite a seven minute mile."

Kids are throwing, pitching and hitting softballs.

Thank goodness I'm not one of them. Thank you Miss Ditch! It's not time to go in yet, so I just keep running.

When Miss Ditch blows her whistle, I keep running off the track toward the locker room. I never imagined that I could actually enjoy a gym class. As we are getting dressed, Miss Ditch yells over the noise and chatter in the locker room, "Panic, see me in my office before you leave."

I can't help but wonder why. *What did I do now?*

A few minutes later, I'm at her door, feeling sick to my stomach. "Miss Ditch, you wanted to see me?"

"Panic, we've been thinking about starting a girl's track team. All the other county high schools compete, and Page High should too. There are a lot of meets left this year. We've already checked with the league and they'll let us participate in them. Wednesday, we'll be doing track events in all our gym classes and choosing the best girls. We won't have a lot of time to practice, but two weeks should give us something. Can I count on you for our team?"

"Me? You actually want *me* on a team? I don't know what to say."

"Well, think about I and talk to your parents," Miss Ditch says.

"Sure, thanks," I say as I turn to leave.

I can hardly contain my excitement! Groovy! *Me* on a track team!

The day passes quickly and I see Annie on the bus, so I sit across the aisle from her.

Annie, You'll never guess what happened in gym class today!"

"You flunked another skills test?"

"No, no, something cool… amazing, actually! Miss Ditch let me get out of taking the skills test and timed me on the track. I almost made a seven-minute mile! And that's not all! Miss Ditch wants me to be on the girls track team!"

"Whoa! Slow down. *You* are running on a track team! We don't even have a girls track team?!"

"Yeah, but Miss Ditch says the school has been talking about it. And the other high schools are okay with us joining them even though it's the season has already started."

"That is so cool! I bet Dad and Mom will be excited too. I can just see the headline in the school paper: 'From Gym Class Klutz to Track Star'," Annie says.

"Ta Da!" I throw my arms up and my head back. "That's me1" I say, grinning.

#

It seems like forever until dinnertime. For once I have some news to talk about and Mom and Dad are late.

When we are all seated, Annie says, "Kennie has some great news! She-"

"Let me tell them," I interrupt as I explode with excitement. Miss Ditch wants ME to be on the track team! Yes, ME!!"

"That's great!" Dad says. "Does this mean that you and Miss Ditch are finally getting along?"

Mom smiles at me.

I continue, "Can you believe that? Miss Ditch let me get out of taking the softball skills test and timed my mile around the track instead. I almost did a seven-minute mile, and she's sure she can get me down to six or even better! It's great to actually be able to do *something* right in gym class! Isn't that amazing? For once, it's good to be small and skinny. With no wind resistance, I don't have to use as much energy as the big athletic kids."

"So, what? What's a track team anyway?" Bonnie asks.

"It's like a baseball or a football team, only with a track team, your score depends on how fast you run, not on how you hit the ball or get it over a line."

"Oh, before I forget," Mom says, "the eye doctor has a cancellation and will be able to see you on Monday, Kenda. Now back to this track team, what does it involve?"

"Well, we have meets at different schools every Saturday, and I'd stay after school a few days a week for practices."

"After school is fine, but *every* Saturday? How would you get there?" Mom asks.

"I'm sure there'd be a bus to take us from the high school."

"And how will you get to and from the high school? You know how busy our Saturdays are." Mom says.

"I don't know," I mumble, seeing Annie's imaginary headline in the school newspaper vanish.

Dad frowns at Mom, then he looks at me and says, "If this is something you really want to do, we'll try to find a way."

"Yes, please, yes! I really, really want to do this!"

30. DASHED DREAMS

Lying in bed, I hear Mom and Dad arguing. Mom's annoyed voice is loud. "I know you are all excited about this track team. But Kennie doesn't really have to do it, and it would be a *big* burden on us. It means driving her back and forth to the high school on Saturdays. You know that's the only time the stores are open when we're not working. We have to get groceries and all the other shopping done, not to mention chores around the house and the gardens. Especially now that it's spring, there's lots of planting, weeding, and watering on top of the cows, chickens, cats and dog."

But Dad defends me. "Oh, Honey," he says, "This is important to her. Kennie really wants to be part of something at that huge high school. This sport would be just the thing! Being part of the swimming and diving team did wonders for me at Curtis High. Smart kids never get the recognition that athletes do. Being shy, little, and lost in the crowd, I think she *should* do this, if for no other reason than raising her self-esteem."

Mom jumps in with, "Yes, but Kennie's not the only one in this is family. We both work long weeks, leave the house at seven in the morning and don't get home until almost six at night. With your night classes, the projects around the house and the farm, we *all* have to work hard on Saturdays to get everything done! It's not just her time, but *someone* has to drive her. And what about those Saturdays when you get called into work? What then? You're always the one talking about being practical. I don't see this as practical or even possible!"

Dad's voice rises. "But she really deserves the chance to do this. Don't you realize how she's picked-on, especially in gym class? Just be willing to give it a try, for her sake."

"I hear you. But I don't know a single person whose life was perfect growing up. I was a nobody, and the dumbest kid in my whole school!" Mom replies.

"This isn't going to make her life perfect! It'll just help her fit in. And she can learn a lot from winning and losing on a team," Dad counters.

"Yeah! But, we just can't disrupt our routine. We need our Saturdays free from chauffeuring her to and from the school at whatever hours for track meets. Why is it so hard to get that into your head?" Mom retaliates.

"I know it would add to our weekend commitments. But, I really think you're being unreasonable. It only takes a half an hour to get to the school. You have no problems with Annie and all the school plays she works on. That gives her a sense of belonging and a group to be part of. We take her back and forth to the dress rehearsals and performances," Dad states.

"That's different. They are all in the evening and only a few times a year, not every weekend all spring!" Mom continues. "Driving her back and forth would mean two hours every Saturday and even more if you are working. I would have to be the one to drive her. With only one car, I just don't see how this is possible."

Dad says, "I wish I could convince you that it would be worth it. But you seem stuck on your position."

"Well, there is no other option. We can't make this commitment. There simply isn't enough time in a Saturday. You'll just have to tell her in the morning."

#

After overhearing the argument, I start to cry and bury my head in my pillow. I am mad at Mom. She'd never do anything *just* for me. She won't even listen to Dad. All that is bad enough. But what on earth will I tell Miss Ditch? Here she's trying so hard to give me a chance, to let me shine in her class. It's going to be like slamming the door in her face! I'll never be able to look her in the eye after this. I should make Mom go to school and tell her why I can't be on the track team.

#

I squint in the morning light. It's a sunshiny day, but not in my world. I move slowly, buried in my own gloom. Everyone is in the dining room when I get there for breakfast.

"Good Morning, Minnie," Dad says with a forced smile.

"You know we are so proud of you," he begins, "and we'd love to see you on the track team. It's just not possible with all our commitments. And I'll be working more Saturdays—"

"—Yeah!" I shout, cutting him off and glaring at Mom. You don't care about me! It's horrible being a klutz. Not that either of you would understand. You danced, Mom, and you were on the swim team, Dad. And now, finally *I* get a chance to do something—to redeem myself from the pit of clumsy, unwanted team players, and you have to ruin it!"

Everyone at the table stares at me as if I were an alien from outer space. But I continue. "If we lived closer to school and had friends to carpool with and didn't have all these chores, I could do it. But NO! You had to move from our nice neighborhood to this stupid farm! We can't be normal kids. Everyone else not only knew what a softball was, but had played the game at their parks. Not me, I'm clumsy and a social retard."

Dad opens his mouth to say something. But I ignore him and keep talking. "When everyone else goes roller skating, bowling and to the movies, we are marooned here with stupid animals and a huge garden. Don't you get it? You are crazy thinking this is a good life. This country-living makes us 'nobodies'."

Even Bonnie's quiet through my outburst. She's staring at me with her eyes about to pop out of her face, and her mouth wide open.

Mom speaks first, "Now, Kennie," she says, "calm down." We are only trying to do what's best for the family. We work hard so that you will never go hungry and fall asleep with frost on the inside of the windows."

"Other kids don't have to live on stupid farms to have warm houses and food on their tables. They don't ever waste hours of their lives scraping chicken poop, pulling weeds, and shelling grocery bags full of lima beans!" I shout as I slam my fist on the table.

"We'll have to continue this discussion at dinner time. We all better get going or we'll be late for school and work," Dad says with a strained calmness to his voice.

We all scatter. I bolt from the dining room, too mad to eat.

#

Walking down the gravelly road to the bus stop, Annie finally says, "Wow! You sure let Mom and Dad know how you feel this morning. I can understand how upset you are about the track team. But I was really surprised to hear you speak up. That was a good thing, even if it seemed a bit disrespectful."

"I don't care. This was my one chance to belong, and it's *just not possible*", I say. "You're in the drama club and work on all the school plays. You have friends outside your classes and you've got a good gym teacher. I guess *you* don't really get it either," I reply, feeling frustrated even with her.

"Besides, I have to tell Miss Ditch! I can't imagine anything worse," I shout.

"Oh just tell her, she won't kill you." Even Annie's annoyed at me.

I start thinking about what I'm going to say to Miss Ditch. Annie and I walk the rest of the way in silence.

#

When I get to homeroom, Mr. LeCourt notices the cloud over my head.

"Kenda, you look like you just lost your best friend. Is there anything I can do?" he asks.

"Yes," I reply. "Make my parents move so I can be on the track team, or at least tell Miss Ditch I can't," I reply.

"Well, I'm not sure it's in my jurisdiction to get your parents to move. Since we can't change that, then you just need to talk to Miss Ditch. Tell her the truth. I don't think the consequences will be anything near as bad as you expect," Mr. LeCourt says kindly.

I try to smile as I thank him for the advice.

When I arrive in the locker room, I go straight to Miss Ditch's office. She's sitting at her desk, stretching her arms.

"Panic, can I help you?"

"I hope so. I hope you'll understand."

"Understand what?"

"That I can't be on the track team." I blurt out.

She tilts her head, frowns and says, "Hmm… this sounds like something we need more than sixty seconds to discuss. Can you come by after school?"

"Yes, of course, Miss Ditch," I answer, feeling relieved.

The day drags on, and my brain is pre-occupied with the after school meeting.

Finally, when the last bell rings, I head to Miss Ditch's office. She's waiting for me, and motions for me to sit down.

Then she asks, "okay, what's this all about?"

The words come pouring out, "You see, we live way out in the country and have tons of chores to do. Mom and Dad both work, so Saturdays are the only time they can shop since the stores are closed on Sundays and when they get home from work. All day Saturday we have to feed animals, make repairs on the chicken coop, plant, water, weed, chop wood and all that awful country-stuff. So there's no way I can get back and forth to the school. It really makes me mad because I would love to be part of a team, and I think I could be a good runner. I'm willing to practice and work hard."

"I have no doubt about that," says Miss Ditch. "I've seen your determination." For the first time she talks to me more like a guidance counselor than a gym teacher.

"You mean you're okay with that? You aren't going to flunk me or penalize me for not taking advantage of the opportunity?" I ask in disbelief.

"Panic, I am really proud of you for coming directly to me and talking about it. You are actually standing up for yourself for change. While I am disappointed, I certainly wouldn't penalize you."

"So you aren't going to keep me after school for more softball practice or anything?" I ask.

"Oh, Panic, you don't get it. It's not about hitting a softball. It's not really about the track team," she says with a bit of a grin.

"What? I'm confused."

"It's about giving you a taste of success, about getting you to believe in yourself, to show some backbone, to be bold," Miss Ditch explains.

"So you *really* don't care about me hitting a softball?" I ask, not sure I actually believe it.

Miss Ditch nods and laughs.

"And as for the track team," I add, "I want to do that more than anything!" I slap my hand on the desk.

“So, Kenda, how can you make that happen?” Miss Ditch challenges me. “Surely you’ve heard the expression ‘Where there’s a will, there’s a way.’”

“Yes, of course,” I say. “So if I’m going to solve this problem, I need to figure out what the obstacles are and then how to overcome them.”

“Now you’re talking, girl!” Miss Ditch encourages me.

“Mom’s objections are transportation on Saturday and chores,” I say. “I can get my chores done by doing a little more after school each day, after the track meets, and even on Sunday.”

“Okay that’s part of it.” Miss Ditch says, leaning forward, as if anticipating my next words.

I put my elbow on the edge of her desk and hold up my head with my left hand. “So I just need to get back and forth to the high school on Saturday when there are no busses.”

There’s a long pause.

“Wait a minute. Bus—that’s the clue. If someone who rides my bus is on the team, maybe I could carpool with her.”

“All right,” Miss Ditch says. “Now who rides your bus?”

“Sharon O’Neil and Linda Lyman.”

“Let me check their track times on the President’s Physical Fitness Tests. If one of them qualifies, then we just might be able to work this out, Kenda.”

Did she call me Kenda?!

31. BEING BOLD

As I get on the late bus, Tom smiles at me and slides over in his seat. I muster my courage and sit next to him.

"Hi! How was debate team this afternoon?" I ask, trying to sound casual.

"You're mighty cheerful today. What's up? You don't look like you've been playing softball or anything like that," Tom says grinning.

"No, but I had a meeting with Miss Ditch."

"And you're smiling and not sweating? That must be a first!" Tom laughs.

"Yes, I went to tell her I couldn't be on the track team. Man, I was dreading it. But it was amazing! Miss Ditch was actually *nice* to me, and she thinks we can work it out," I explain.

"So what were you afraid of? The worst thing that could've happened was that she got ticked off at you. So what? You take your ten minutes of deep grief, and then it's over."

"That seems so logical now, but I worried all day," I say.

"I'm glad it turned out well. Maybe next time you won't waste energy on something that might not even happen."

Tom's smart, and not just when it comes to schoolwork.

"Thanks for the advice," I say. "So you never told me about your debate team meeting," I add, eager to turn the conversation away from me.

"Oh yeah, you did ask me about that. We didn't have a meet today. I talked to our sponsor. It's never been this hard to debate an issue for me. I'm supposed to take a stand against civil rights. Now, most of the time I can see both sides of an issue."

"So this is different?" I ask.

"I really believe in equality. Discrimination still exists and it's *wrong*," Tom says.

"You don't have to convince me." I reply.

But he continues talking about colored folks being people too, about how wrong slavery was and how it lives on.

"Time to go!" Tom jumps up, grabbing the books in his lap, and turning to get past me.

When he looks back to say goodbye, he waves with a smile on his face.

I wave back, grinning inside and out.

#

All afternoon as I do my chores, I'm thinking of Tom and of our conversation. Wow! He's really smart, cares about people, and he's handsome besides. With his blond hair, bright blue eyes, and broad shoulders, he's a real hunk. It took a bit of nerve to make myself sit next to him on the bus, but once I'd done that, talking was easier. I need to stop being afraid, of expecting the worst. I could make my life so much better, if I start being bold as Miss Ditch says.

The sound of car tires on the gravel pulls me out of my wonderful daydream. Mom comes in the door first, her hair drooping and her shoulders sagging. Dad doesn't say anything and moves slower than usual. Even Bonnie isn't bouncing around.

"Hey, y'all, what's wrong?" I ask.

"As if you don't know how badly your outburst this morning made us feel," Mom says.

When we are at the dinner table, Dad finally speaks.

"Kennie, we can understand your disappointment about the track team, but that was no way to talk to us this morning." Dad's tone is serious.

"I'm sorry about getting so angry. But I meant *every* word I said! My life is the pits. You didn't spend your life doing farm chores when you should have been socializing."

Bonnie asks, "What's socializing?"

"Making friends and doing fun stuff together," I answer, while Mom and Dad just look at each other.

"Kennie, we're sorry you feel that way. But, this is our life, and you'll just have to learn to make the best of it. You can decide where to live when you make your own money and raise your own kids wherever you think is best." Dad looks me in the eye as he talks.

"What about making my life better *now*?" I ask.

"And how do you propose to do that?" Dad wants to know.

"By fitting my chores in during the week, after track, and on Sundays." I reply. "And I've also got a plan to get to the school for track meets."

Annie moves her head from me to Dad and back again, as if her eyes are following a ping-pong ball moving back and forth across the table.

"Okay," Dad says. "What's the plan?"

"I think I might be able to get a ride with another girl on my bus. If that works out, can I be on the team?" I plead.

"Hmm, I think we could go for that. We should pay whoever drives you something for the extra gas and their time." Dad seems like he's buying my solution.

"I still have all my money from tutoring," I add quickly before money becomes an issue. "I don't mind spending that if it means I can do track."

Dad looks over at Mom.

"That's fine by me," Mom says, as she nods her head. "Kennie I have to hand it to you for figuring this out for yourself."

32. THE EYE DOCTOR

Mom pulls up to Bonnie's pre-school on Monday Morning. Bonnie slams the door. Mom and I are alone in the car, just the two of us.

"Mom, how old were you when you first got glasses?" I ask.

"I was seventeen. I always got headaches when I tried to read. About the tenth time I came to class without my reading assignment done for English, my teacher sent me to the eye doctor a block away from the school." Mom adjusts her glasses as she speaks.

"Your Mom didn't take you?" I ask.

"Oh, heavens, no," Mom replies. "She worked as an aide at the hospital during the day and the rest of the time, she was at the pub with my step-father."

"So, she didn't pay for your glasses *either*?" I ask.

"I paid for everything I needed with the money I made working at the drugstore soda fountain after school. I even paid for a lot of things for my sister and brothers," Mom explains.

When we get to the eye doctor's, a pretty lady with long wavy hair greets us from behind a counter.

"Hello, Mrs. Pannek," she says. "And you must be Kenda."

"Good Morning, Laura," Mom replies, as Laura hands her a clipboard.

I watch her fill in the form in her beautiful handwriting, until Laura calls for me to follow her.

She smiles and opens a door to a long thin examining room that's painted a light blue with a large black leather chair at one end. Next to the chair is a long robotic arm with a machine that has two eyeholes. At the end of the room is the standard eye chart with random letters, each row a little smaller than the one above it.

A cheerful, tall, thin man walks casually toward me as he buttons his white coat.

"Hi, I'm Dr. Hand. You must be Kenda. Pretty name," he says as he extends his right hand toward me.

"Yes, pleased to meet you." I answer politely and shake his hand.

By pretty name, he means pretty unusual, I think to myself.

"So what brings you here this morning?" he asks.

"I can't see the board in English class," I reply.

"Have you ever had glasses or an eye exam?" he asks.

"No," I answer.

"Well, let's get on with it," he says as he hands me a black plastic thing with a handle and a large circle on the end. He tells me to cover my left eye. I proceed to read almost all the way through the lines on the chart across the room.

"All right, then cover your right eye."

I cover my eye and read the first letter, then the three on the second line, and try to make out the four letters below that.

"Okay, keep going… the next line."

"I can only make out blobs, not really any letters."

Dr. Hand pulls a small cardboard page suspended from a thin metal arm in front of me.

Can you read this? The print gets smaller and smaller as I go down the page. He takes my chin and gently moves my head to the left. The writing becomes much harder to read. I slow down and stumble on easy words. Good grief, even a third grader could read better than this.

"That's all right, try covering your right eye."

When I put the plastic thing over my eye, the print clears up again and I am able to read much better.

"Okay, let's try the other eye."

Now I really struggle, it's like the ink has become pale and I have a hard time even seeing the words.

"It looks like you are myopic in the left eye and hyperopic in the left," Dr. Hand says.

"What does that mean?" I ask.

"To put it in regular English, nearsighted and farsighted. When did you first start having trouble seeing?" he asks.

"I just noticed it last week when my English teacher moved me to the back of the room."

Next he pulls the machine with the holes in front of my eyes and starts the quiz.

"Which is better? One or two? How about now? One or two? And so on."

Sometimes, it's hard to tell, they are about the same.

"Do you realize you're using your left eye almost exclusively to read, and your right eye for distance? Don't you have vision screens in school?" Dr. Hand asks.

"Yes, but I always remember all the letters on the chart when I read them with my right eye. They never ask us to do anything close up, so I never flunked an eye test," I tell him. Then I ask, "Why do you think I use only my left eye to read? I can see out of my right."

"First of all, you tilt your head so the left eye is in a direct line with the print. Secondly, your brain is not processing what you see very well with the right eye. I'll bet you don't read much for pleasure."

"No, not at all," I answer.

He writes some numbers on a piece of paper and hands it to me.

"Take this out to Laura and pick out some frames with her." Then Dr. Hand gives me a firm handshake, saying, "It was nice to meet you, Kenda."

As I go over to the wall of eyeglass frames, Mom joins me.

I try on a pretty pair of copper-colored frames. Mom looks at the price— $120.

"Out of the question," she says.

So I start checking the price tags and finally find a pair of thin black plastic frames that we can afford. These are okay and they aren't so thick that they make me look nerdy. Mom nods.

I bring them to Laura's counter and she writes up a card, which she gives Mom. Then Laura tells us she'll call when my glasses are ready.

Fumbling in her purse, Mom takes out her checkbook. After she hands the check to Laura, we say good-bye.

When we get in the car, I thank Mom, lean over and give her a hug. She puts one hand on my shoulder and pats my arm with the other.

"I wonder how long you've had trouble seeing," Mom says.

I wonder what it really means to be nearsighted in one eye and farsighted in the other. I wonder if that explains why I could never hit a softball. It actually seemed to disappear when it was coming toward me and I never had a clue how far away it was.

"Probably forever," I say. "I just thought that was normal."

33. TRACK PRACTICE

As I snap up my gym suit. My mind goes back to all the days I dreaded walking into the gym for this class. Today is different. Miss Ditch is going to announce the girls who made the track team. For once, I might feel like a hero.

"Time's a wastin'! Everybody out in the gym!" Miss Ditch shouts.

We line up for exercises. I am in the far back, as usual. But I decide to ignore the eight counts and do two-count jumping jacks. No one seems to notice. At the end of warm-ups, Miss Ditch pulls a paper out of her pocket.

"All right, girls, listen up," she says. "I'd like to announce our Girl's Track Team. These selections were made based on running times from your Physical Fitness Tests."

The gym is quiet. All eyes are on Miss Ditch. She scans down the paper as she says, "Let's see, first period, there are four of you in here. Poison, Lyman—"

Girls nod their heads and smile in the direction of Renee and Linda. A few hands begin to clap.

Miss Ditch raises her voice and continues. And our Co-Captains, Nick and Panic."

Mary Sue stretches her eyes at me, and her mouth drops open. The gym is silent.

"Believe it or not," Miss Ditch announces, "Panic had the best time in all the track events, except the fifty yard dash. When it comes to running, she can hit it out of the park!"

Girls are clapping, cheering, and shouting my name. My face turns red, and I grin.

"Okay, to the track!" Miss Ditch shouts as she motions toward the outside door. The stampede begins, as everyone rushes into the sunshine. Mason comes over and pats me on the back. "Good goin'," she says. "You deserve a break in here."

"Yeah. I guess it's about time." Mary Sue adds.

I raise my eyebrows and snap my head back to see her face. Mary Sue nods and smiles.

"What a terrific day!" I say, as I breathe in the warm air and run to the track.

When class ends, I can't believe that I actually enjoyed gym class.

Back in the locker room, Miss Ditch blows her whistle to get our attention over the chatter and slamming lockers.

"One more thing," she says. "The four of you on the track team need to be here for practice at 3:05, dressed and ready to run."

At lunch, I'm sitting with Sally, Margy, Sharon and Erik. Kids I barely know are coming over to congratulate me.

"I bet Mary Sue quits picking on you now," Erik says.

"I wouldn't count on it." I reply. "But maybe you're right. She was nice to me after she got over the shock of it."

"Wait until I tell Tom," Sharon says. "He'll be so happy for you. Especially since he knows what you went though with softball."

#

The day flies by and soon there are twelve of us out on the track.

Nick says, "I'll lead us in the exercises and Panic can take over with stretches."

After that Miss Ditch pulls out her stopwatch and we run, and run some more. It's easy to get lost in the rhythm of sneakers hitting the track in the warm sunshine. I'm not the only one who forgot the time.

Miss Ditch blows her whistle. Then she shouts, "Girls, hurry, it's almost four o'clock! No time to change clothes."

We race to the locker room. My lock sticks. I try the combination again. Still, it won't open. I need my books and purse out of there. Finally it lets me in, and I grab my stuff.

The locker room is empty. I run down the hall and out the front door, just as my bus pulls away. Waving an arm, I try to get the driver's attention, but he's already driving down the street.

I hang my head. Now what? I guess I have to call Mom or Dad. I trudge back into the building and walk to the counter in the office.

The secretary looks up and asks, "Can I help you?"

"Yes, I need to use the phone to call my Dad. I missed the late bus."

She pulls a black phone from under the counter and sets it in front of me.

I fumble through my purse, find the number and dial it.

Dad's secretary answers on the first ring, "Federal Aviation Agency, Mr. Pannek's office. May I help you?"

"Could I speak to him please?" I answer. "This is his daughter."

"He's out in the radar building," she says. "Is this an emergency?"

"No, not really." I say. "I just missed the late bus, and I need him to pick me up at the high school on his way home."

"I can certainly tell him when he comes in. But he probably won't be leaving for at least another hour. So you'll have to wait quite awhile for him."

"That's okay. I can go in the library and do my homework," I lie.

"All right," Dad's secretary says. "I'll be sure he knows."

Then I call Annie and tell her, just so she won't be worried, or call Mom at work and tell Mom I'm not home yet.

I go to the nearest Girl's room and change my clothes and then I head back outside. I sit down on the steps. It's way too pretty to be cooped up in the library. The sky is bright blue with a few wispy clouds. A couple of kids are holding hands as they walk along the sidewalk. A girl is coming toward the school, carrying a red sweater. She looks familiar. But that green blouse and madras plaid skirt could be anyone. It's hard to make out her face because she's looking down at the ground. As she gets closer, I'm sure it's Mary Sue. She doesn't even see me. She wipes tears from her cheeks with the back of her hand. Her face doesn't look bruised. Should I say something? What *should* I say? Will she get mad and tell me to mind my own business?

"Mary Sue?" I whisper, just loud enough for her to hear.

"Uh?" she turns her head.

"Mary Sue, what's the matter?" I ask.

"I lost it. I lost my mother's locket," she says, touching her neck and moving her hand down toward her heart.

"It must be very special if you're this upset about it," I say. "I can help."

Mary Sue stops and looks at me. "Wait, what are you doing here?"

"I missed the late bus. I've got an hour to kill," I say. "So tell me what this locket looks like and how you lost it."

"It's silver and about this big," she answers holding her thumb and index finger about an inch apart.

She continues, "I know I had it on when I left the meeting. I was so happy that I got an afternoon work placement at the *McLean Providence Journal*. I was rubbing the locket then. I walked out of the building and was almost home when I realized it was gone. I've re-traced my steps all the way back to here."

"So let's start here and go back into the building." I say opening the front door to the school. I turn to wait for Mary Sue to come. She's looking to the side of the steps. I let go of the door.

"My chain," Mary Sue says bending down and picking it up. She holds it in the palm of her hand. It's broken.

"The locket must be close if this is your chain," I say getting down on my knees and sweeping my hands in the grass.

Mary Sue is next me. A ladybug crawls up onto to my finger.

"Hmm. Ladybugs are supposed to be lucky," I say.

"I'll believe that when we find the locket." Mary Sue says, stretching her neck to look at me. Then she moves backwards on her hands and knees.

When I move over to the right, I get a shooting pain in my knee. I reach down to rub it and there's the locket in my hand!

"Mary Sue, is this it?"

She comes over and carefully takes it. She holds it in the palms of her hands like a tiny egg that might crack, and she starts to cry.

"Mary Sue, why are you crying?" I ask. "We found it. Your Mom won't be upset at you, now."

She shakes her head and sits down on the step.

I sit next to her and put my hand on her shoulder.

"Kenda," she sniffles. "You don't understand. My Mom's dead."

I stare at her. "What?"

"Yeah, My Mom died. She had lung cancer. The doctors said it was because she smoked too much." Mary Sue is talking softly, more to herself than me. "It was the year after my brother, Johnny, died in the car accident. Dad and I tried to take care of Mom. Our lives fell apart."

"Oh, Mary Sue! I'm so sorry!" I say.

"I missed so much school I had to repeat eighth grade. Dad couldn't preach anymore. He couldn't understand how God could take away both Johnny and Mom from us. They got another pastor, and he used up what little savings we had, but he couldn't pay the mortgage. Dad got a job at Sears, sold the house in our old neighborhood, and managed to get the little one here by the school."

"That's really sad," I say.

"Actually, Dad and I are okay now. After he got rid of Rod, we both feel lucky to have each other."

"And I thought *my* life was the pits," I say. "Speaking of luck, do you believe in ladybugs now?"

Mary Sue chuckles and smiles at me.

EPILOGUE

Mary Sue stopped smoking, graduated, got married, and had two sons. She finally had to divorce Craig because his nightmares and drinking got to be too much. She would sit and write in her journal after the kids went to sleep and before he came home from the bar. Mary Sue landed a job writing for the *Washington Post*. She wrote a book about World War II and her characters came from those Craig described, the ones that haunted him. The difference was that the World War II soldiers were heroes—those who fought in Vietnam were spit upon when they came back. Mary Sue and her kids moved in with her father who was a wonderful influence on them. The older boy, Zach, helped to fill the hole left in her Dad's heart from Johnny's death so many years ago.

Kenda went on to graduate school and got a Ph.D. in biochemistry. She did cancer research at the Mayo Clinic. Luckily, she didn't have to pass years of physical education skills tests to graduate, or she would have been a high school dropout.

Miss Ditch is still teaching at Page High School. Although she's mellowed a bit, she's still tough and challenges all her students, demanding they stretch themselves to the limit. She had to drop the track team, because there was no money for uniforms or busses. (Sports and higher education for girls were not considered important in the 1960s. Title IX, which ended gender discrimination, did not become a law until 1972.)

Tom never realized his dream of becoming a lawyer. He drew a low lottery number in the draft and was killed in Vietnam.

Erik became a stonemason and built patios, walls and walkways for many beautiful mansions around Washington D.C.

ABOUT THE AUTHOR

Carol Lynn Luck (a.k.a. Carol Lach) was the high school English student who hated to write, as she felt she had nothing to say. Her PhD in the sciences taught her to think critically and she published many articles in scientific and educational journals in her 50 years after high school. Upon retiring, she realized the richness and variety of the nine lives she had spent in scientific research, teaching, marketing, technology, parenting, management, entrepreneurship, education and caregiving.

Her first novel, *Heroines of the Kitchen Table* tells about four young women who defied Hitler and struggled to save their loved ones. Through the years, Carol had heard their stories over kitchen tables. This is different from most Holocaust novels in that it tells the story from five different perspectives. She has started her next novel, *The Day the Chalkboard Fell,* which is based on teaching experiences in Mississippi the year the schools were forcibly integrated.

Carol lives in Framingham Massachusetts with her husband. She especially enjoys visits from her two kids. Carol is passionate about providing a meaningful public education that allows all children to reach their full potential.

Visit her website at www.CarolLynnLuck.com .

ACKNOWLEDGEMENTS

This novel began as stories I related to friends in Wisconsin. One of these friends, Suze Timmel, repeatedly told me I needed to write a book. About 30 years later, I found myself in a writing class in Massachusetts with an incredible instructor, Carrie Johnson. She told us to write about what we knew—great advice! Carrie's encouragement upon hearing me read episodes contained in this book gave me the confidence to believe that I had what it takes to become an author. There are not enough words of appreciation for these two friends.

Linda De Cougny and Matt Osber loved the scattered episodes I shared, and made me feel obligated to put them all together. Early drafts were long and included far too much back-story. Nonetheless, Paula Fillion, Jane Holzapfel, and Nicole Savoie slogged through them. Their suggestions, edits, and words of encouragement motivated me to persevere. Paula convinced me that the messages in the book needed to be told. Holly Smith was a great pre-reader and made sure I kept true to the times.

After substantial revisions, friends from the Writer's Loft in Sherborn made important contributions that helped Kenda grow up. I am most grateful to Lisa Kramer and Vanessa Wright. Warren Ross and Thea Iberall pushed me to give the reader my best.

Miriam Glassman, my wonderful editor, gave me the courage to cut whole sections of the original manuscript. She uncovered discrepancies like the best of detectives, and sleuthed out a lot of grammatical and structural issues. Without Miriam's hard work, this book would have been terribly boring and Kenda would not have become the person she did.

There are not enough wonderful words for my husband, Ben, and my kids, Lisa and David. They gave me time and space to write and encouragement to persevere. Thank you for being my best cheerleaders!

LETTER FROM THE AUTHOR

Dear Reader,

Do you know what it's like to be the last one picked for a team or to be excluded from a group? Like Kenda, I sure did! Some kids belonged to their own exclusive cliques. Others felt we had little in common and just ignored me. There were a few who started out as archenemies, but circumstances provided opportunities for understanding. Out of that grew kindness and compassion. It is my hope that, even in the age of cell-phones, you will find time to just hang out and talk with others, especially those you may not like at first glance. Who knows, like Mary Sue and Kenda, you may be surprised how understanding leads to laughter, compassion and maybe even friendship.

You have probably known a Miss Ditch or a Mr. LeCourt. I am thankful for many great teachers who knew their subjects and taught them with passion. They expected our best efforts, and communicated well. Most important, these great teachers really cared about us as individuals. This book is dedicated to all the wonderful teachers who help students earn self-esteem through grit and perseverance.

In looking back 50 years, I was lucky. The mission of education was to help students find a passion, and offer opportunities for them to master the skills they needed to transform that passion into a career. Unfortunately, now the focus is on standardized test scores, rigorous graduation requirements, and a college degree. The educational system assumes that one size fits all. The Mary Sues of today won't graduate because they need four years of high school math. It is my hope that this book may influence educators and policy makers to return to providing a meaningful education for all students.

Thank you for picking up *Gym Class Klutz.* I hope Kenda, Mary Sue, Miss Ditch and the others brought you a few laughs, a sense of school in the '60s, and a little wisdom.

All the best,

Carol

ONE LAST THING…

If you enjoyed this book or found it educational, entertaining or otherwise useful, I would be most grateful if you took a few minutes to post a short review on Amazon. These reviews matter. I read each and every one personally and your feedback can make this book and my future novels even better.

Thank you so much for your support,

Carol Lynn Luck

www.CarolLynnLuck.com
@luckwrites
Facebook.com/Carol Lach

Made in the USA
Middletown, DE
29 April 2016